Praise fo

"Some events left me speechless and utterly in shock (I'm still trying to get certain scenes out of my mind). Five stars for a read that had me up all night and watching comedy movies for a few days after."

—Horrorigins on *The Portal*

"James creates powerful intimacy and terror…a seriously creepy page-turner that will keep readers up all night."

—Publisher's Weekly on *Q Island*

"James has a talent for combining action-packed vignettes into a powerful, fast-paced whole."

—Library Journal on *Black Magic*

James elevates this above similar efforts. The result is a thrilling game of supernatural cat and mouse.

—Publisher's Weekly on *Demon Dagger*

"This short novel is chock full of action, perfect for horror fans who like their reads quick."

—Booklist on *Demon Dagger*

Deeper into Darkness

Russell James

MLG Publishing

Contents

Extra Play When Lit

"So, this is the place my grandfather told me about."

Stewart Dixon gritted his teeth at the disappointment in the young deliveryman's voice. This unappreciative, sun-bleached surfer stood inside Rhapsody Mansion. Didn't every red-blooded male dream of walking these halls?

The *LA Times* had called Rhapsody Mansion "The House that Porn Built." Of course, back then the *LA Times* had readers and porn hadn't turned into amateurs humping on cheap websites. In its prime, Rhapsody Mansion had been the home of Stewart Dixon and his merry-go-round of young starlets. Movies made in the basement beneath, hedonism practiced in the rooms above.

"Where do you want the crate?" the deliveryman said.

"Put it in that corner," Dixon answered. "Watch the tools on the floor."

Dixon pointed his withered, shaking hand to the far corner of the room. The years had faded his papery skin to near transparency, save the splotchy liver spots. His comb over of sparse, gray hair didn't even fool himself anymore. Any semblance of muscle tone had long ago departed, like the entourage that used to populate the mansion.

The room had been called the Playpen in its day, and still wore the décor of that time, like a stooped dowager forever dressed in her debutante gown. Overstuffed white couches bracketed tables of glass and tarnished chrome, overseen by kitschy ceiling lamps that recalled bad modern art. A full bar covered one wall. A white marble mantle framed a gas fireplace filled with cracked and rusting metal logs. Dust motes floated through the stale, still air.

Dixon's portrait hung above the fireplace, a gaudy oil version of him in his prime, forty years younger, in a red smoking jacket, two nude women at his feet wearing looks of adoration. Now his flowing brown locks and the girls in the painting were long gone. He thought he had the smoking jacket in a box somewhere.

The deliveryman put his shoulder against the shipping crate and rolled his hand truck into Dixon's appointed vacant corner. He pulled back the hand truck and left the box against the wall. It looked like an L lying on the long side.

The deliveryman slipped off his black hooded sweatshirt, and took a power screwdriver from the tool pile to the packing crate. He pulled off the top first, reached in, and retrieved a piece of paper. He looked at it, shrugged, and handed it to Dixon. Dixon inspected it.

BLASTS FROM THE PAST
Relive your youth with items from our vast collection.
Pre-war to present. Locator service available.

Handwritten underneath it read:

Enjoy your gift!

The deliveryman removed the last few screws. The sides fell away and revealed the precious cargo within, a gleaming pinball machine.

"Whoa, a major antique," the deliveryman said.

Dixon pushed past him and shoved a fifty into the man's hand. The deliveryman uncrumpled it. His eyes went wide.

"Anything else you need done around here?"

Dixon waved him off toward the door without even a glance. The man sighed and left the room, hand truck in tow behind him.

This model pinball machine, the Lucky Ace, had been state of the art when it rolled out of the assembly plant in 1962. In the upright backglass art, two improbably buxom women in vintage Daisy Duke-attire bracketed a suave, tuxedoed player at a poker table. Four aces and a king lay before him beside a pile of chips. A lit cigarette hung from the corner of his sly, victorious smile.

In the play area, twin banks of triple flippers lined the sides of the machine. Four pop bumpers crowded the center. Slingshot kickers stood sentinel throughout the playfield. Thirteen pop-down tabs arced around the upper left side, painted like a full suit of spades, ace up to king. Smack all thirteen of these with the same ball and the phrase beneath them, *EXTRA PLAY WHEN LIT*, glowed bright red and the player earned another ball.

The email announcing this gift had amazed Dixon. Fans of the now defunct *Rhapsody* magazine had sent him this as a token of appreciation for years of illicit arousal. The skin mag had pushed the boundaries until they broke, usually with under-age girls he'd pinned with fake birth certificates.

Dixon leaned against the base of the machine. He caressed the edges with his wrinkled, tremulous fingertips, then rested them within the familiar indentations of the flipper buttons. He sighed.

The collectors prized this rare model for its unique, offset-triple-flipper design. But this groundbreaking experiment enabled such extended play, that the model was discontinued when playtimes rose and revenue dropped. But Dixon's elation at the announcement of the machine's impending arrival was personal. The Lucky Ace had been the machine at the rear of Enzo's Pizza.

Enzo's had been Dixon's favorite hangout during his lonely high school years. In the rear of the strip mall establishment, he had lavished rolls of quarters and hours of time on the game. Back in the day, he'd mastered this machine, understood how to vary the compression on the plunger for a perfect launch, knew just the right pressure on the flipper to smack the ball into the target of his choice, and could finesse a two-handed nudge to just under the machine's tilt limit. Only he had ever rolled over the six-digit counter.

And of course, he'd dreamed of becoming old Lucky Ace, suave and debonair, surrounded by women ready to put out. He'd grown up and lived that dream, and unfortunately, continued a few decades beyond it.

Stevens, Dixon's burly, clean-cut, head of security entered the Playpen. The creases in his dark suit looked like they could cut paper. Even indoors, he wore his Secret Service-issued sunglasses.

"Sir," Stevens said. "The delivery vehicle is clear of the estate."

Stevens gave the pinball machine a quick inspection, more like sizing it up as a potential threat than an aesthetic evaluation. Then he resumed his usual stiff, modified military stance, and looked straight ahead.

"See what this represents?" Dixon said. "*Rhapsody* fans still remember who the skin king is. It's not even my birthday."

"It looks like it makes you happy, sir." Stevens' expression did not change.

"Why don't you get the hell out of here, and make sure the front gate locks behind that truck."

"Yes, sir."

Stevens retreated, and closed the door behind him. Dixon checked his reflection in the backglass, superimposed over the self-assured poker player. He'd seen himself there hundreds of times before, a few inches higher, face fuller, eyes brighter, hair far longer and much darker. But old Lucky Ace hadn't aged a day, the smirking bastard.

Dixon tapped both flippers twice. The machine awakened like the comatose to consciousness. The upright backglass lit life into the three faces there. Pop bumpers dinged and turned bright white. The score counter rolled back to zero in a grinding symphony of tiny bell rings. The cabinet hummed in his hands.

Dixon stepped away in surprise. The machine went dead. He peered underneath between the legs. The plug lay on the floor like a road kill snake. Goosebumps crawled up his arms.

"It's converted to battery power, or it's some greenie-weenie solar thing," he muttered. Neither of the rationalizations made much sense. The idea of the machine running without power filled him with wariness. But at the same time, whatever power lit those bumpers also lit the desire in him to play.

He placed his fingers back on the flipper controls. The machine revived. A familiar progression of three bell notes sounded, a musical phrase Dixon hadn't heard in an eternity, though once it had been part of his life's soundtrack. The two low notes followed by one very high was the Lucky Ace's call to arms, the announcement to let the games begin.

On the playfield beneath the thick, clear glass, the pop bumpers flashed. Red and blue lights flickered behind the various extra point scores. In the backglass, a bulb backlit the card player's eyes. The lines of smoke from his cigarette seemed to waver.

Dixon touched the flippers. They fired, smooth and swift. A silver ball popped out of a chute with a sharp crack against the cover glass, and rolled into position against the plunger. The ball shimmered like mercury.

Dixon grasped the plunger handle. The arthritis in his fingers ground like sandpaper between his joints. He pulled the plunger back and released.

The ball travelled two-thirds of the way up the delivery chute, slowed and rolled back down. It bounced once on the plunger's rubber tip, and lay still.

"Damn," he said to himself. "You've become one lame-ass son of a bitch."

He gripped the plunger handle again. He pulled back farther, this time adding his shoulder's protests of pain to those in his hands. He released the handle.

The ball sailed up and out of the delivery chute like a satellite launch. It entered the maze of upper bumpers, and let loose a cacophony of bells and a flurry of flashing lights. The ball rocketed across the playfield, dropped the tab carrying the six of spades, and ricocheted to the right side, dead on target for the center triple flipper.

Dixon hit the button. The flipper sent the ball back up the playfield where it hit the deuce of spades, and sent it down out of sight.

Dixon's eyes glowed like one of the extra score lights. A pulse of adrenaline primed his flagging heart.

The ball bounced down in a straight line to the space between the final flippers. It sailed through the gap. Bells rang. The score counter spun and clicked over a new total.

"Son of a bitch." Dixon had always hated those straight drops through the center.

The machine coughed ball number two up to the plunger. Dixon sent the sphere flying. He hunkered down over the machine, squinting against the ravages of age upon his eyesight. He watched the ball the way a stalking lion tracked a flitting gazelle. This play lasted longer. He downed half the suit of spades. A bad bounce sent the ball through a side gate. The scoring numbers cartwheeled over 50,000. Ball number three popped up for play.

Dixon's legs quivered. One at a time, he raised a knee and wiped his damp palms against his pants, afraid to release the controls and have the machine drop dead mid-play. He took a deep breath to steady himself.

"Goddamn. Winded playing pinball. Dix, there was a time you could bang chicks for hours on end and not break a sweat."

He wiped his brow against his shoulder, and then let the last ball fly.

Dixon's long term memory resurrected his dormant flipper skills. Points racked up. He soon downed the full suit of cards, save the three of spades.

He averted a disaster with a one-two tap on the lower flippers, and sent the ball up the playfield. It smacked the three of spades head on.

The card dropped. Bells rang like a carillon gone mad. *EXTRA PLAY WHEN LIT* blazed in fiery crimson. The full suit of cards popped back up, daring a second decimation.

"Yeah!" Dixon's pulse thumped. He pounded the flippers in victory, even though the ball bounced in play between the pop bumpers. He teetered on the tips of his toes.

He racked up another few thousand points before the ball disappeared through a side gate.

He shivered in exhilaration over the high score. Then he realized it wasn't the score, which was just a fraction of his youthful all-time high. It was the extended play win, the accomplishment of downing all thirteen cards and the reward of another ball that had pumped him up.

He reached down to launch the final ball. He gripped the plunger without a trace of discomfort in his hand. He flexed it once, twice. Pain free. He inspected it, and while it might have been his imagination, he could swear that the liver spots on his hands had faded.

He finished the last ball of the game. The counters finally stilled and the *GAME OVER* light announced the end of play. The bulb behind the poker player's eyes flickered as if he winked.

An addictive desire for a second game infused Dixon. He hadn't needed a quarter for the first one. Hell, he hadn't needed electricity, but that odd little incongruity had faded away completely. He tapped the flippers twice. The score counter rolled to zero. The three bells announced a polished silver pinball's return to launch position. Old Lucky Ace smiled.

Dixon played a second game, then a third, and then lost count. With each ball, his timing improved, his feel for the game sharpened. He saved questionable rebounds. He picked and hit his targets. Each game's score rolled higher than the one before.

"Mr. Dixon?" Stevens called from the doorway.

The interruption broke Dixon's concentration. He flubbed a shot and the ball dropped down the middle.

"Damn it!" he said. "What?"

He didn't turn around, afraid to break his grip that kept the machine alive.

"Just making sure everything is okay before passing it to the night shift, sir. I mean, given the time."

Dixon leaned over to check his gold wristwatch. Seven at night? He'd been playing for hours.

"The kitchen wondered about your dinner, sir."

He wasn't the least bit hungry. "Dismiss them."

Stevens retreated and pulled the door shut behind him.

Dixon inspected his hand again. The spots *had* faded. No more than the first time he'd checked, but he was certain of it now. And there was no question that the joints in his fingers were less swollen, less painful.

He tapped up another game. The first two disappointing balls barely scored a point. The third ball was charmed. He didn't miss a shot. Bumpers rang, targets dropped. The suit of spades vanished one by one, until only the queen remained. Dixon caught the ball on the right upper flipper. He let it roll down to the tip and tapped the button. The ball sailed up and nailed the queen.

EXTRA PLAY WHEN LIT turned scarlet. The adrenaline surge swept through him again. A chill shivered up his spine. His shoulders warmed from the inside. He could practically feel the osteoarthritis there melt away.

By the time *GAME OVER* lit again, instead of sagging under the weight of the late hour and the fatigue of play, he stood invigorated.

He smiled at his reflection in the backglass, a smirk that mirrored the card player's. Dixon's eyes widened. His image was crisp and clear, as it had looked before time had stiffened his eyes' lenses. The wattle of flesh beneath his chin had shrunk. The lines around his eyes were finer. He looked closer at his doppelgänger. He stretched his neck. It wasn't just the lighting. He'd changed.

The last thing he believed in was magic and all that supernatural crap. But there was no denying that the more he played this game, the better he felt, the younger he became. Knocking down the suit of spades turned back his clock. Extra play indeed.

Oh, to turn back the clock. Back to when his pecker stood high and hard without a dose of Viagra. Back before amber alerts and the kiddie cops looked for every damn runaway that came to LA, back when he could convince those doe-eyed waifs that their path to stardom started by kneeling in front of his fly.

Maybe this was his ticket. With the knowledge he had now, with the Internet to leverage, and with a dozen foreign countries without child-porn taboos, he could turn his millions into billions this time around. If he could get this machine to turn the trick, he'd have the time, and the energy, to build the biggest empire yet. He just needed to roll up a few extra plays on this machine. And he wasn't going to waste time letting luck play any part in it.

He released the machine. It fell dark. He picked the electric screwdriver up from the floor, and spun the screws out of the glass cover over the playfield. The machine wouldn't stay on without having his hands on the flippers or plunger, so he couldn't just start a ball with the glass open and tap down the playing cards. But he could sure as hell improve his odds.

He grabbed a napkin from the bar and wadded it into a ball. He reached in and shoved it down into the hole between the bottom flippers. He stuffed other napkins in the side gates. He'd only need one ball to turn back his clock.

He lowered the glass back into place. He rubbed his hands together, and then blew on them. The air conditioning clicked on and the vent swept cold air across the back of his neck. He winced. He wasn't going all the way upstairs just to get a sweater. The deliveryman had left his hoodie behind. Dixon put it on and popped the hood up over his bare neck.

He touched the flipper controls with both hands. The machine blinked to life. Lucky Ace gave him his knowing smile. The counter reset to zero. Dong, dong, ding! A ball popped up against the plunger. Dixon pulled it back and fired.

Shooting fish in a barrel never felt so good. Dixon literally couldn't miss. Ricochets and rebounds sent the ball spinning across the playing field in a dizzying, non-stop journey. Bells dinged like angelic machine gun fire. A lightning storm of lights flashed. Playing cards dropped, *EXTRA PLAY* went ruby. The fire of youth flowed back through Dixon's veins.

The cards reset and Dixon knocked them down, two, three more times. His exhilaration surged with each victory, his arms grew stronger, his legs less tired. His reflexes sharpened and even without the cheating napkins, he rarely flubbed a rebound. The score counter never stopped moving.

Ace, six, four, jack. Bam! The cards popped down, and then jumped back up again. Dixon practically danced behind the machine as he fired one flipper and then the other. Dreams of his future empire, and the pliant girls who would populate it, flashed before his eyes. And the girls would be even more pliant this time. Instead of alcohol and pot to lubricate the process, he'd employ the big timesavers of roofies and crystal meth.

The ball hung in an extended score-spinning dance between two pop bumpers. Dixon caught a quick glimpse of himself in the backglass. The hood shadowed much of his face, but his smile shone though, white and straight, like it used to be, just across Lucky Ace's neck.

The door flew open. Dixon spun around at the intrusion. The machine went dead as his hands left its sides.

Harris, the night shift security, entered, fury in his eyes. Harris had been in the NFL for four years before landing this job, and hadn't lost a degree of his ability to intimidate. The shoulders of his suit coat barely cleared the doorframe.

"What the hell are you doing in here?" he bellowed.

"Who do you think you're talking to?" Dixon chopped the last word short. His voice was high, reedy, unfamiliar.

Harris grabbed Dixon at the shoulders. His meaty hands practically crushed Dixon's slender joints. Harris lifted Dixon off the floor and shook him.

"Kid, I don't know how you got past three levels of security, but it's gonna be the biggest mistake you ever made. Who's here with you?"

"No one, you idiot. It's me, Stewart Dixon. What's wrong with you?"

Even as he said it, Dixon knew the question was backwards. There wasn't something wrong with Harris. There was something wrong with him. The narrow shoulders, the high voice, the loose fit of his clothes. What had this machine done to him?

"Playing smart ass, huh?" Harris said.

He dropped Dixon to the floor and then grabbed him at the collar hard enough to make him choke.

"I ought to call the cops, but I don't need to play a game of Twenty Questions about how you got this far into the building on my watch. Stevens is itching for an excuse to can my ass."

Dixon choked out a protest. Harris swung him away from the pinball machine, and dragged him, back-first, through the Playpen door.

As he passed through the threshold, the light behind the card player's eyes flashed once, and old Lucky Ace winked him goodbye.

◆◆◆

Harris pushed the button to roll open the mansion's front gate. It slid left with a clatter of the drive chain. He dropped his death grip on Dixon's collar. Dixon wheezed in relief.

"Not only are you fired," Dixon gasped, "but I'm going to sue you—"

Harris swung an underhand punch up into Dixon's breadbasket. Dixon's lungs compressed. He dropped to the ground. He sucked in one jagged breath just in time for Harris to give him a savage kick that sent him up in the air and rolling out the main gate. He thumped to a stop where the driveway met Foothill Road.

"Catch you in here again, kid, and you'll get worse than that, and a ride with Beverly Hills' finest. Now crawl back under whatever rock you came from."

Dixon flipped on his back against the gutter. The gate ground closed and Harris walked away. Dixon stared up at a blurry night sky. Something inside him felt swollen, damaged. He vowed to ruin that prick guard's life for good.

Then he wondered how. He had no ID with him. He looked at his hairless arms, felt his smooth cheeks. He hooked his thumb in his belt loop, and pulled away his loose waistband. Not a hair between his legs. He was a boy. The damn machine had rewound him just a little too far. How was he ever going to explain this?

He reasoned that he could use his fingerprints, his DNA. Then he realized that neither of those were on file anywhere, having never had a brush with the law, or a passport.

A white Camry pulled to a stop on Foothill Road. A woman in her fifties exited the passenger door. She ran to Dixon's side.

"Oh, my God! Are you all right?"

Dixon coughed and wiped his mouth. No blood. That was probably good news. He nodded that he was okay.

The woman's black hair had a marginal dye job and was cut too short for Dixon's taste. Her mom jeans and simple, long-sleeved T-shirt screamed that she was at least one kid's grandmother. Shock and compassion filled her eyes.

Excellent, he thought. However he was going to get this sorted out, he wasn't going to get it done out here on the street.

"What happened to you?" she asked as she knelt beside him.

"A couple of kids jumped me, took everything I had."

"You poor boy. Why don't we give you a ride home?"

Dixon stood slowly. The beating made him feel as old as he'd been a few hours ago.

"Thanks, ma'am." If this lady could get him down to Marina Del Rey, he could board his yacht, and start to sort things out.

The woman opened the door for him. With a low moan, he settled into the cheap cloth back seat. Another auburn-haired woman about the same age sat behind the wheel. She eyed Dixon from the rearview mirror. The Good Samaritan got in. The driver's eyes flicked away from the mirror, and the Camry pulled away from the curb. The rear doors locked.

"Thanks, ladies," Dixon said. "My name is—"

"We know your name, Dix," the passenger said, voice hard as steel. "Don't you know ours?"

A chill ran up Dixon's spine. This situation suddenly felt catastrophically wrong.

"Should I?"

The passenger turned around in her seat. Her face looked vaguely familiar, but not at this age. Something about her eyes…

"I'm Kara Hill, this is my sister, Britney."

She pulled up the sleeve of her shirt and exposed an irregular trail of small circular scars up her inner forearm.

"When we were fifteen and sixteen, the three of us and a pack of cigarettes played a very painful game."

Dixon's stomach dropped to the ground. Kara and Brit. Fresh off the bus from Asswipe, Oklahoma. They spent a few months at the mansion in a drug-induced haze before he kicked their spent, scrawny asses to the curb.

"Look, ladies, I don't know what you are talking about. I was walking home from school, two kids jumped me—"

"Stuff it, Dix. We sent you the Lucky Ace."

Dixon abandoned his pretense. "You?"

"Well, not just us. We had a lot of help, a sorority of victims, victims of you. It takes a pretty big coven to cast a spell as powerful as the one we put on that pinball machine. Not to mention how long it took us to find the specific stupid model you always talked about."

"You did this to me?"

"No, jackass, *you* did that to you. That's the beauty of it. We cast a good spell to reverse the aging process. We might have made the acceleration rate a bit steep after the first extra play, but we'll draw no repercussions for using dark magic. We knew with your greed and physical deterioration, you'd hit it like a pig to a trough.

"But we were nice enough to put in a limit. We stopped you at age twelve, instead of letting you send yourself back to wearing diapers. Or at your age, were you already wearing them again?"

Dixon bristled at the taunt. His dick might not have been sexually able on its own, but it still pissed fine.

The car passed out of the tonier residential areas and swung south on Western, deeper into Los Angeles.

"We were out here waiting for the cops to arrive. We figured your security would have them arrest a kid who broke into the Rhapsody Mansion. We were going to follow you to the station and bail you out. But scraping you off the street after getting the shit kicked out of you was a lot more rewarding."

Kara laughed without mirth. Britney sent another silent, burning stare back via the rearview mirror.

They turned left off Western. The neighborhood around them began a slow deterioration. An increase in graffiti, a decrease in working streetlights. Furtive young men tried to keep to the shadows near street corners.

"Look, Kara," Dixon said. He assumed his sleaze-tinged version of charm. "Your visit here was a long time ago. It was a different age. We were all young, just having fun—"

"Fun?" Kara practically spat out the word. "You call defiling, damaging and abandoning girls fun, you sick bastard?"

Dixon gripped the front seat back in frustration.

"Well, the joke's on you and your pack of psycho witches," Dixon said. "Because I'm young again, and rich, and this time around, it'll be no holds barred."

"Oh, you're young, all right. And you're going to stay that way. You'll be twelve years old forever. You might die of something else, but it won't be old age."

A look of horror crossed Dixon's face. Kara's lit up.

"Yes, you just got it. You'll never see puberty, never be sexually capable, for the rest of what we hope will be a long and wonderful life."

The car slowed for a curve. Dixon grabbed the handle and yanked. The locked door didn't yield. He pounded the unlock button to no effect. Sweat peppered his forehead.

Kara pointed the barrel of a pistol into the back seat.

"But we didn't want you to go through life unloved," she said. "We're not *evil* witches."

The car rolled to a stop. The door locks popped. Dixon grabbed for the handle, but the door opened before he could pull it.

A ponytailed Mexican man stuck his broad face into the car. A star tattoo adorned the skin above his right cheekbone. Three tattooed tears ran down from his left eye. He smiled and revealed two gold incisors.

Dixon's heart stopped. Everyone with any connection to the skin industry had heard of Benito "Big Dog" Estevez, the king of catering to pedophiles. Kara jammed the pistol barrel into Dixon's side to hold him in place.

"Hey, boy," Big Dog said. His breath smelled like cigarettes and cheap booze. His skin shined like a snake's. "I got a line of new friends waiting for you inside already. You gonna be very popular."

♦♦♦

This story was inspired by a trip to the Pinball Hall of Fame, a big warehouse in Las Vegas filled with working pinball machines the owners actually let you play. The story was supposed to have a happy ending, but one thing led to another and...

Ω

My Soul Is in the Theater

Each evening, the stage at the Barclay Theatre overflowed with life. The actors that trod upon its boards and the resounding applause of the audience infused it with vitality. But this morning, without that energy, the silent building slept away its idle hours.

Jackson Breen had the theater to himself. He stood center stage, tall and angular, sporting the goatee grown for his lead role. He wore blue jeans and a black t-shirt, an anachronism among the nineteenth- century furnishings on the set of *Orchids in Bloom*. His black leather jacket lay across the couch. With the curtains drawn and the stage lights down, he could see the thousands of orchestra section seats, the hundreds more on the balcony. Empty, they looked so strange. The play had sold out every performance.

Jackson breathed in the invigorating, unique smell of a theater stage. Along with the usual aromas of makeup, sweat and burning gels, the Barclay carried the veteran scent of age. The fragrance of dried wood and musty curtains reminded each actor that others had walked these boards for over a century. It was a welcome change from Jackson's usual Hollywood movie set, now mostly sterile rooms wallpapered in green to accommodate special effects.

He took a seat in the overstuffed leather chair his character favored throughout the play. Enthroned on it each night, he felt the power of the patriarch he played flow through him. But now, in the dim light, out of costume, without an audience, he was just a man in a chair, no different from perching in a dentist's waiting room.

Something moved in the shadows at the stage's far end. He tensed. Even he wasn't supposed to be here at this early hour. He stood with the hope that his six foot height might add a level of intimidation. It wasn't necessary.

Kelly Connor stepped out from the wings. She wore a tight-fitting set of pants and a V-neck blue t-shirt under an open camel's hair trench coat. Tall and rail-thin, she had the perfect build for the play's period costumes. She looked quite contemporary with her short wedged blonde hair, so different from her appearance each night in a black wig with a bun. She grinned at Jackson like a kid caught swiping cookies.

"I thought the only person I'd run into before noon would be a janitor," she said. "You haven't picked that up as a second job, have you?"

"Couldn't," Jackson said. "I only work Equity gigs."

She took a seat in the Queen Anne chair across from Jackson, the same chair she occupied for half the play. She looked beautiful, as always, but perhaps because they were both out of character, she didn't send that tingle up Jackson's spine like she did during their scenes together didn't charge the electricity that powered the depth of his performance.

"So what brings you to the Barclay so early in the morning?" he asked.

"Gratitude," she sighed. "Wonder. Bewilderment. All of the above." She gave her head a slow shake. "The show is just the hit I need."

Six months ago, conventional wisdom had declared Kelly's Broadway career dead. A disastrous combination of drug abuse, slurred performances and diva behavior had earned her a pink slip from the prophetically titled *The End of Miracles*. Months of West Coast rehab declared her clean, but she was still a risk. She jumped at the chance to play opposite Jackson on *Orchids in Bloom*.

"You have been magnificent," Jackson said. "You deserve every note of praise the critics sing."

"Part of that is your responsibility," she said. "From the first rehearsal, your performance has brought out the best in mine."

"I feel the same way," he said. This wasn't the usual mutual admiration society ego stroke all actors offered each other. Jackson had made films with Oscar winning actresses. He'd never felt a connection with a leading lady like when the curtain rose at the Barclay each night.

"I'd been away from a live audience for years, doing movies and TV," he continued. "I can admit now that the prospect of theater kind of scared me. Every scene suddenly had just one take. No one could save me in the editing room. Working without a net, so to speak."

He swept his arm out across the sea of open seats.

"But it's amazing," he said. "I'd forgotten the energy of the audience, what it does for my performance. I think my soul is in the theater after all."

They both sat for a moment lost in their own parallel thoughts.

"I was third choice," Kelly said.

"Come again?"

"Two others turned down *Orchids in Bloom* before they offered it to me," she said. "They loved the part but wouldn't work in the Barclay."

"Superstitious fools."

"You don't believe the stories?"

"Oh," Jackson said. "I believe that Emma Moore and Billy Faustino committed suicide on stage here in 1890 when their play closed to the world's worst reviews. The tragic lover's tale is almost too much to believe, but I've seen the old newspaper headlines.

"Do I believe the silly stories about haunted spirits stalking the backstage? Nonsense. I haven't seen anything supernatural transpire and neither has anyone else. What I *do* believe in is the Barclay's string of successes. The list of careers made and remade at this venue is as long as my arm. That's the kind of mojo I buy into."

"So instead you think the theater is magic?"

"Well, no. I think that the audience was predisposed to see excellence based on the theater's history of hits. I think that positive energy brings out a great performance. And I say our results validate that theory."

"Who am I to argue?" she said, tossing her hands in the air. "Maybe it's you, maybe it's the play, maybe it's the stage, maybe it's the alignment of the stars. All I know is that I hope it lasts several hundred performances."

◆◆◆

That night, Jackson and Kelly stood in the wings and waited for their entrance cue. Jackson wore the heavy layers of velvet and starch that guaranteed a hot night under the spotlights. Kelly was coiffed and corseted into the personification of a Gilded Age matriarch, down to the matching parasol.

Jackson wrung his hands. By now, he had always stepped into the life of Chester Ellington, oil baron, and felt the authority of the man flow through him. Tonight, he just felt like an actor dressed as a fool.

He looked at Kelly. He didn't feel the magic. That singing in his heart that he heard when he stepped on stage with her hadn't begun. He gazed at her profile against the cluttered backstage backdrop. She didn't shine as she had each night before. She didn't look like the elegant Mrs. Ellington, tycoon's wife. She looked like Kelly Conner in thick stage makeup.

Kelly's eyes darted back and forth across the stage as the supporting cast worked the first scene. A bead of sweat rolled out from under her thick black wig and down past her left ear. Her lower lip trembled.

She's lost it too, Jackson thought. His heart ran in his chest like a jackrabbit. She's nervous. Weeks of perfect shows and she's nervous. We jinxed it! We talked about the craft, tried to dissect it, and overanalyzed the whole thing. Now we're both lost, two people about to parrot memorized lines back and forth for two hours before a bored, silent audience.

Seconds remained to their entrance. And the end of their careers.

◆◆◆

A man and woman leaned against a table of props offstage behind the two leads, in the stagehands' area clear of the actor's paths.

"I felt the urge again," the man whispered, voice tinged in sadness. "That wanderlust or whatever it is."

"The feeling that it's time to leave the Barclay?" she said. She looked past the waiting actors at the action on the well-lit stage. "Like you've had before?"

"Stronger this time," he said. "We've worked this venue for so long…"

"…that it feels like a prison," she finished. "I know. I felt the same way all week."

The man peered around the edge of the curtain at the packed house. "This place does pull in the crowds. But I've got this longing to move on."

The audience roared with laughter at a well-delivered punch line.

"Where will we go if this is the last night we work the Barclay's backstage?" the woman said.

"I'm not sure," he said. He managed a weak smile. "It's the way of the theater. You never know what the next gig will be until you land it."

"What if in our next gigs aren't together?"

The man turned to face her. His mouth fell.

"We would have to be together. That's a given."

"And if we aren't?"

"We'll come back to the Barclay."

"If we can," she said.

The man hung his head and stared across the table full of props. Offstage, Jackson gave his tight collar an annoyed tug. Kelly patted away sweat from her brow.

Relief lit the man's face like a marquee. "Then we stay. Whatever adventures await elsewhere can wait a little longer. In fact, they can wait forever if we risk experiencing them apart. I'll fight the wanderlust if you will."

Her eyes twinkled as she smiled

"As prisons go," she said, "this one's not bad."

"Here comes our cue," he said.

They walked up behind Jackson and Kelly. The man reached out without thinking to caress the woman's shoulder. His hand passed through her. He laughed at himself for still forgetting after a century.

"I love you, Emma," he said.

"I love you, Billy."

"What's out there that could trump sharing the stage with you?"

They both stepped forward into Jackson and Kelly and disappeared.

◆◆◆

Jackson's heart skipped a beat. His skin flushed. He turned to Kelly. Her eyes sparkled like sunlight on diamonds. That familiar shudder surged up his spine. Kelly smiled at him, relaxed and confident.

"Knock 'em dead, Kell," he said.

"Every night," she replied.

An actor on stage gave their cue. They entered stage right and hit their marks. The crowd erupted in applause.

♦♦♦

My wife asked me why I never wrote a story about nice ghosts. Now I have.

Ω

Stone Cold

"This is so exciting!" Trina said.

Roland couldn't say he agreed. Crystal Caverns looked like a hole in the ground from where he stood. Worse, it looked like a tourist trap hole in the ground, and not even a first-tier one.

If nowhere really did have a middle, this place could well have been it. Crystal Caverns lay about twenty well-wooded miles off I-65. Its weedy gravel parking lot sat at the end of a dirt road. Three dilapidated log cabins lined one side. On the other stood a sagging office/ticket booth. From the woods between them rose the black entrance to the cave; a low, narrow passage into a stone hillside, ringed with flowering kudzu.

"I don't know how you found this place," Roland said. "There isn't a word of advertising anywhere. Not even a *Turn Here* sign."

"Dubbya dubbya dubbya dot roadside treasures dot com," Trina said. She whipped her long black hair back into a ponytail. "And it's half way to Gulf Shores!"

"So are a lot of other places," Roland said. He eyed the dreary cabins. "Places with hot water." He tapped his darkened cell phone. "Places with cell towers."

Trina faced him and tugged down the corners of his Ohio State t-shirt over his belly. She rubbed her hand over his buzzed brown hair and made a mockingly sad face.

"Aw, just one day off campus and already lost. Will you survive a whole week of Spring Break?"

He batted her hand away. "I was willing to drive straight through and avoid re-enacting a scene from *Deliverance* out here in Nowhere-ville."

"You're a geology major," Trina said. "This should be fun for you."

"I've seen caves rigged up for tourists," he said. "The damage to the formations makes me cry."

She wrapped an arm around his waist and looked up with those big brown eyes that he fell in love with last month.

"Well tomorrow afternoon it will be all beach, bikini and beer," she said. "Just to make it up to you."

He kissed her. "You'd better."

"Last tour, y'all!" announced a man by the ticket window.

"C'mon!" Trina spun around and took Roland in tow. His heart skipped a beat as he caught a glimpse of the tattooed strand of ivy that peeked out from the feathered edge of her short shorts.

They fell in behind a half-dozen other visitors, all dressed in high-tourist fashion. All eyes were glued to the man in khaki shirt with a Crystal Caverns patch over his right pocket.

He couldn't have been past twenty and was hard scrabble-country thin. His shaved head was shaped like a light bulb and when he opened his mouth, the view of his jumbled teeth within made Roland's jaw hurt.

"Now y'all step up. My name's Cal. This here's our last tour for the day, last chance to see the amazin' wonders of Crystal Cavern. Just five dollars a head, three for kids."

With no children in the group, Roland wondered why he mentioned it.

"Ooh, my treat!" Trina said as she whipped out a ten. She handed it to Cal. He smiled his cluttered smile and nodded them forward.

The group followed him down a thinly mulched trail to the cavern opening. Just inside the kudzu curtain, a heavy iron gate blocked their entrance.

"Gate here's two-fold," Cal said as he pulled out a single black skeleton key from his pocket. "Keeps the curious youngsters out and keeps the cave gnomes in."

Roland exhaled a resigned sigh as his worst fears about this adventure were realized. But half the group chuckled. Cal brightened like he'd gone over big at The Laugh Factory.

"Just kidding, just kidding," he said.

He stepped inside and threw a big power switch on a wall circuit box. Twin trails of floor-level lights flickered on. They bordered a tight curved path that snaked away between the narrow walls.

"Crystal Cavern's been in the family since near forever," Cal said. "First tours were done by lantern light before the War Between the States."

They followed Cal down the dim passageway. The air turned cooler and damper with every yard. The passage narrowed and a more rotund couple had to physically squeeze between two boulders. Roland was behind them and feared he might have to give the husband a little shove to help him through, but his wife pulled from the other side and he popped out like a champagne cork.

Cal tossed out some other cavern facts about length and width and depth. His deep accent and the constant echoing combined to make him incomprehensible.

A few hundred yards in, the claustrophobic passageway opened up to a large cavern. The visitors gasped. Poorly placed colored spotlights could not distract from the formation's natural beauty. Delicate, thin stalactites hung from the high ceiling, many several feet long with a single bead of water clinging to the tip. Wider, more irregular stalagmites rose from the cavern floor like a standing-room-only concert crowd.

Roland had to admit some of the more remote, less disturbed formations were in pretty good shape.

"Now these take decades to create," Cal said as he led them down a path between the stalagmites.

"Seriously?" Roland said under his breath. Geology apparently wasn't part of Alabama high school curriculum. These formations took millennia to create, one drip of water at a time leaving a microscopic deposit of minerals.

"Some folks claim to see things in the shapes," Cal continued.

"Oooh, this one looks like a bird," the fat woman said to her husband.

He huffed in return. Roland inspected it as he passed and agreed with the husband.

"Rollie, look here," Trina said.

She stood in front of one larger formation. An inverted crescent covered it about chest high.

"It looks like a person's face," she said. "See the frown, the eyes, the nose."

"C'mon, Trina," Roland said. "They probably carved that in there to make the place more interesting. Cal practically pointed it out to us."

They passed several other formations. Roland noticed their relative human height and some vague facial features, clearly all carved fakery. Typical of what people, unchecked by scientific appreciation, did to caves.

Trina looked increasingly scared as she looked upon each formation. At the end of the cavern, the group paused around Cal. He stood next to two switches atop a peeling wooden pedestal.

"And here you see a very special formation," he said.

He flipped one switch and illuminated a large granite stone shaped like a squat mushroom. One side had a pronounced droop.

"This here's the Home of the Gnomes," Cal said. "The cave gnomes live inside here, only coming out in the dark. But don't worry none, these here lights will keep them at bay."

Roland shook his head.

"Their sworn duty," Cal continued, "is to protect the crystal treasure."

He threw the second switch. A spotlight lit the wall behind the stone mushroom. White quartz crystals protruded from the wall at odd angles. They sparkled in the floodlight.

"In olden days, folks would venture into the cave and chip the crystals from the wall. The gnomes would leave the cave at night, and drag the thieves back. They would cast a spell and the thieves became the formations you see here." He gestured to the stalagmites with a poorly choreographed sweep of his hands.

"So the gnomes stopped when people stopped stealing the crystals?" the fat woman asked.

"No ma'am," Cal said. "The gnomes found they had a taste for it and started to kidnap regular visitors. Anointed 'em with a drop of cave water and then tracked them down that night. That's why we had to put up the gate."

Trina screeched. Roland whirled to face her.

"Trina?"

Water glistened on her forehead. "Water! Dripped right out of nowhere. Right on me!"

"It just dripped from the ceiling," Roland assured her. "Don't get spooked by all this nonsense."

"Looks like the gnomes have selected another one," Cal announced.

Trina rubbed her forehead like she was putting out a fire.

Roland turned back to Cal and had to restrain himself from punching him in the face. "You aren't helping here, buddy."

"Sorry, sorry," Cal said, hands raised in submission. "Sorry, ma'am. Just funning with ya." He turned to the rest of the group. "That's the tour folks. Back up to the daylight."

◆◆◆

The two of them lay staring at the cobwebbed ceiling from the bed in Cabin Two. Cheap paneling covered the log walls. The tiny, ancient water heater took up precious space in one corner. Their bags were still in the car. There was no table or dresser to put them on and the filthy floor was out of the question. A nightstand lamp marginally lit the room through a yellowed lampshade. Roland's unfulfilled dream of Trina's sexual conquest remained just that.

"I can't believe that you let that stupid hick's story get under your skin," Roland said.

"For the hundredth time, the water dripped on me right after he said the gnomes worked that way. Coincidence?"

"Well, yes."

"Did you get dripped on? Did anyone else get dripped on during the tour?"

"No, but there was a lot of dripping. The floor was wet everywhere."

"But only on me."

He wrapped an arm across her waist. She stiffened.

"Look, I'm beat," he said. "I drove all day on no sleep. Let me get a few hours in and we'll blow out of here before dawn, okay?"

"Promise?"

"Absolutely." He snapped off the light, yawned and closed his eyes. "Bright and early…"

◆◆◆

Roland woke up freezing cold. He shimmied over to be closer to Trina. He reached the other side of the empty bed. He bolted upright.

"Trina?"

A cold wind blew in and ruffled the covers on the bed. The cabin door yawned wide open. Absolute darkness covered the parking lot outside.

Roland leapt out of bed and jumped into a pair of pants. He ran out to the parking lot. Gravel dug into his bare feet.

"Trina! Trina!"

Deafening silence answered his calls. He looked into his car's windows in case she'd opted for back seat sleeping. Empty.

He rattled the doors of the other two cabins. Locked. He ran to the office and pounded on the door. No answer. She sure wouldn't walk off into the woods. Where else could she...

He looked over at the entrance to the cave. One flickering footlight lit the entrance. The gate was open.

"Oh, hell no." She'd gotten herself so spooked that she went into there? That didn't make sense. Neither did the other option, that gnomes had dragged her in.

He picked his way to the cave entrance. Dry pine needles pricked his toes. A bush rustled in the darkness.

"Trina!" he called when he reached the open gate. Her name had an ominous, hollow ring as it echoed down the dark passageway. "Trina?"

He threw the big switch. The footlights flickered on. The scuttle of scurrying feet sounded from the cavern's far reaches. A muffled voice sounded from far away. His imagination overpowered reason. He dashed into the cave.

He wriggled through the tighter passages that conspired against him. The rough walls scraped his hands as he rushed to rescue Trina from whatever held her captive in the cavern's depths.

He burst into the main room. The lights were on. Trina stood facing the crystal wall.

"Trina!"

He ran straight for her through the maze of damp stalagmites. Two steps from her side, his feet jerked to a stop. He looked down.

Glowing kudzu vines wound around his ankles. The lines ran taut back to the base of two stalagmites, each held tight by a foot-tall, scrawny, sharp-faced gnome. The hairless, naked creatures had long pointed ears and faces more dragon than human. They yanked on the vines and smiled with yellow pointed teeth.

Two more luminous vines flew up from the ground and wrapped around his wrists. The vines drained the strength from his body, pulling energy from his core and out through his hands and feet. Two more vines wrapped around his neck. Gnomes appeared all around him.

"Trina!" he gargled against the constricting vines.

She turned to face him. A gnome hopped up on a stalagmite and jumped to her shoulder like a pet parrot. It chattered something unintelligible. Trina smiled at Roland. The ivy-like tattoo on her leg sprouted a new leaf.

"I guess you believe me now," she said. He voice had a new-found Southern accent.

Water splattered on Roland's head. Cal stepped out of the shadows.

"Nice work, Sis," he said. He turned to Roland. "See, told you about them gnomes. They can't really leave the cave, but they do only come out after sundown. Actress Sis jus' had to bait you down in here somehow."

Roland's wet hair stiffened. Water drips ran down off his shoulders and left sandstone trails. Wet splotches of skin on his face turned rock hard.

"If we give them a sacrifice once per year," Trina said, "they get to do their thing and we get one more treat for the tourists." She giggled. "The irony of picking a geology student, well, how could I resist."

Roland tried to speak but his cheeks already felt that they were encased in plaster. He mumbled something frantic. Trina kissed her finger and put it to his lips.

"Think of it as being part of our family. Welcome home."

Owing to a lot of underground limestone, northern Alabama has a host of cavern attractions, some public, some private. While on a tour of one, water dripped for the ceiling onto my shoulder, and the idea for this story came alive.

Ω

Double Occupancy

"Don't worry, Mother," Lauren said. "I'll take care of everything."

The shifting colors of the city's harsh commercial lights lit the cab's interior as it whisked down 49th Avenue. Lauren tightened her bun of black hair, jarred loose for the hundredth time on this long day of travel. She straightened her heavy thick-framed glasses and caught her reflection in the cab's bulletproof plastic divider. Her despised glasses aged her well past her twenty years.

"You'll take care of it the way you took care of our trip here?" her mother sniped back. "Good God, I was on Amtrak." Mrs. Catherine Van Cleve hadn't traveled in less than airline first class in thirty years.

Mother stared out the cab window and appeared unimpressed by New York's evening bustle. She wore a dark black pants suit and a pair of ankle length black Coach boots with flawless four-inch heels. A small black brimmed hat sat on the back of her head with an attached lace veil draped down across her face. She had adopted this 1940's throwback, along with her white silk gloves, to hide the accident's scars.

"Mother, I told you," Lauren said, "the train would be better than flying with your wheel chair." Perhaps the fifth argument about this would be the one she finally won.

"I'll be the judge of what's best."

Lauren knew her mother couldn't. Mother was consumed with denial. The car wreck had immobilized her from the chest down, but her stubborn New England genes continued to refute that her wheelchair was an impediment. Bulky, certainly, but nothing the world couldn't rearrange themselves around. Apologizing to strangers for her mother had become second nature the past six months.

The cab slowed to a stop in front of the Kensington, the venerable Art Deco masterpiece. The driver stopped the meter and cast an apprehensive glance into the rearview mirror.

"You don't want no help do you?" he grunted.

His attitude inspired Lauren to demand his assistance, but the aftermath would be unbearable. It was acceptable if Lauren lifted her mother into her chair, just a daughter's duty. But if a stranger so much as opened a door... Mrs. Van Cleve would sit quietly during the perceived offense, a passive participant, until she was again alone with Lauren.

"How could you let that man treat me like an invalid? I don't want any man touching (my chair, myself, my clothes...fill in the blank). No one dares affect such familiarity with a Van Cleve."

The firestorm would flare until her mother lost the energy to keep it kindled. Lauren was not in the mood for it after enduring the close confines of the train.

"No, we won't need any help," Lauren said to the driver. He sighed and relaxed behind the wheel. The trunk lid popped open and Lauren shoved the fare into the partition drawer. Buttoning up her navy wool trench, she stepped into the evening chill. She pulled the folded wheelchair from the trunk and snapped it open with one practiced motion. She wheeled it over to the side of the cab and opened her mother's door.

"Here we go, Mother."

Her mother didn't say a word or flex a muscle as Lauren lifted her up and into the wheelchair. Through the short transition Mrs. Van Cleve maintained the haughty bearing of an Egyptian queen being moved to her sedan chair. Lifting her took little effort. Since the accident, her mother, already tennis-club-set thin, had lost more weight, as her muscles atrophied.

Lauren straightened her mother's veil and rolled her towards the brass and glass doors of the Kensington. A doorman in a long maroon coat adorned with gold buttons and piping pushed open the front door. He tipped his matching cap in a casual salute.

"Good evening, ladies," he said. He glanced past Lauren in that fleeting way men always acknowledge plain women. He looked down at her mother. His face twisted into a mix of inquisitiveness and shock. Lauren had grown to expect it when the boorish met her mother. He recovered his bearing quickly. "Any bags, ma'am?" he asked Lauren.

"Two in the trunk please," she answered. She pushed her mother past him and into the lobby.

Lauren's last visit had been so long ago, that then she had to hold her mother's hand on the way inside. The lobby hadn't changed since. The lobby probably hadn't changed in decades. Rose-hued marble floors stretched across the foyer and down the long hallway to the rear. An enormous chandelier held dozens of bulbs that lit the room with a soft light. A set of overstuffed velvet chairs flanked a long-sealed fireplace with a mahogany mantle. The faint sweet smell of fading day-old roses wafted from a table vase. The only soul to be seen was a perky young woman with close cropped red hair behind the check in desk. She typed with intensity at a keyboard in front of a monitor. Lauren stopped her mother short of the counter.

"Mother, I'll check us in," she said.

"Get us a *decent* room," Mother said. "Something with a proper bath and a view of the street. I don't want some tenement dweller ogling me out his bathroom window."

Lauren gritted her teeth into a forced smile and approached the clerk.

"We have a reservation," she said, and slid a credit card across the desk. "The name is Van Cleve."

The clerk tapped a few keys. "Here it is." She noticed Lauren's mother. "The reservation doesn't request a wheelchair access room."

"We don't need one," Lauren said. "I take care of my mother's needs. We need a room with a bath tub and windows that face the street."

The clerk gave Mrs. Van Cleve an odd glance, then punched at the keyboard. She made some swiping motions and passed Lauren back her card and a room key.

"Room 704. The elevators are to the left. If there is any service we can provide, please dial zero and let me know."

Lauren was sure her mother would have a long list as soon as they got to the room. Extra blankets. A late night snack. A replacement for the bottle of shampoo she was certain the last guest had opened.

Lauren wheeled her mother into the waiting elevator. A bellman arrived with their two suitcases. He gave a quick look at Mrs. Van Cleve, and then snapped his eyes back to Lauren.

"I don't want to crowd you," he said to the half-empty elevator. "I'll follow you up on the next trip."

Lauren pushed the "7" button and the doors rolled shut.

"Did you see how that man looked at me?" Mother said. "Like I was some circus freak."

"Mother, he was just…"

"And you let him do it!" she continued. "You stood there like the dim little fool you are, and let that oaf stare at me with those beady eyes. How could you do that?"

Mother gave the wheelchair a sharp spin and a footrest creased Lauren in the shin. Pain sliced up through her leg.

"Ow! Mother!" she cried. Lauren hobbled backward and grabbed the wheelchair's handles. The idea of ramming the chair into the closed doors flashed through her mind. She swallowed hard, and the doors slid open on the seventh floor.

The room met her mother's two stated criteria. A tub and a view. A single king size bed and a plush couch faced the carved TV cabinet. The door to the bathroom was hidden down a short hall. By New York's standards, the room was quite large and well appointed. But to Mother…

"God, what dreadful curtains," she said, pointing at the yellow draperies on the single window. "No wonder this floor looks like a cathouse from the street."

"Mother, let's get you into the bathroom to freshen up," Lauren said. She left the front door open an inch. She spun the wheelchair away from the windows and into the bathroom.

Behind her, the bellman inched the door open.

"Your bags," he announced to the empty room. It came out as a half question.

"Just leave them there," Lauren said from the bathroom doorway.

The bellman leaned in and slid the two bags across the floor, as if some dark force would suck him in if his whole body crossed the threshold. He pulled the door shut behind him and he hurried back downstairs. Lauren shook her head, and turned back to her mother.

The white tiled bathroom had just enough room for the wheelchair. Lauren slipped by and stood in the tub to face her mother. She lifted Mother's veil.

"Now let's touch up your makeup before dinner," Lauren said. She pulled some mascara from her purse.

"Spare me your attempt," Mother said and slapped the mascara away. "I can do all that myself, and far better than you ever could. Look at yourself. After all the money I spent sending you to fine salons, what did you learn? You look positively shopworn."

Lauren involuntarily checked herself in the bathroom mirror. She did look pale, and dark circles bloomed like black algae under her eyes. This trip had been no picnic. The train ride had been tedious, even with a private room, and the constant hammering from her mother hadn't lessened the ordeal any. Perhaps if she'd had a free moment to herself, she could have applied a little something from Estee Lauder. But...

"Don't worry, Mother," she said. "I'll spruce up as soon as you're finished."

"You can't let yourself go like this," Mother said. "It's not becoming a Van Cleve."

The phrase made the hairs on Lauren's neck bristle. How long had that "unbecoming" list grown now? Girl Scouts, track and field, skirts above the knee. As a girl, Lauren wished for a look at the short list of what *was* becoming to a Van Cleve. It would have saved her a lot of grief

Lauren turned her mother to the sink. Mother blotted her face with the tip of a white washcloth. She recoiled at the cloth's unrefined texture and gave it a disdainful look. She reluctantly continued to pat the dirt of the trip from her face.

"I must say," she said. "I think it's your declining appearance that drove away that nice boy you were seeing."

Like a dentist probing a rotting tooth, Mother found Lauren's most vulnerable spot. Lauren's heart pumped faster. She grabbed the end of the shower curtain and twisted it into a ball around her fist.

"Since when did you like Terry?" Lauren asked. Terry had been in her freshman Lit class, and they had started dating a few months before the accident. Terry had made Mother's list between Girl Scouts and short skirts.

"Dear, I'm sure he was as good as you could do," Mother said. "But you've gained five pounds and you dress like you shop at Wal-Mart. Even *he* had to have higher standards than that."

Actually, Lauren had met all of Terry's standards. He weathered every storm, and boosted her over every obstacle. In the dark months after the accident, he'd been the lone light of hope. For Mother to imply that he shared the shallow Van Cleve human grading scheme...

The percolating rage within her went to full boil. Lauren tore the shower curtain off the rod. Broken plastic hooks hit the floor like machine gun fire. She spun the wheelchair back to face her. "How dare you!" she screamed. "Terry was wonderful. He stood by me through the accident's aftermath."

"Don't raise your voice to me, young lady," Mother returned, words cold and hard as steel. "I am your mother."

"Well, I've had enough of this shit," Lauren said. Mother registered no shock at this uncouth profanity. Just a faint arching of one eyebrow.

"That's the type of mouth that drives suitors away," Mother said.

"No!" Lauren said, slamming her hand against wall. Anger flowed fast. She kicked the tub with a hollow boom. "He loved who I was!" She nearly shrieked the words, riding a cleansing eruption of pent-up rage. "But the more I had to care for you, the less he could stand what I became."

"Pardon me for being disabled," Mother said. "But it's your fault I'm in this contraption. You were driving."

The sound of twisting steel and the stench of spraying gasoline flashed through Lauren's memory. Unjustified guilt washed over her. Acid oozed from her stomach ulcer.

"The other driver ran the light. It wasn't my fault."

A sharp prolonged rapping came from the door.

"Ms. Van Cleve?" It was the desk clerk's voice.

"Now look what you've done," Mother hissed.

Lauren squeezed past the wheelchair and bolted to the front door. She gave her hair bun a tightening twist and rubbed her eyes for some composure. She cracked the door with the security chain attached.

"Is everything all right?" the clerk asked. She tried to peer around Lauren's head to check the room.

"We're fine." Lauren forced herself to act collected.

"We had a call about yelling and loud noises. May I come in?"

"Not now. My mother is dressing. Everything's fine." Lauren shut the door and threw the deadbolt.

"See what's happened now?" Mother called. "Your ranting has roused the neighbors. Another mess you've gotten yourself into. Could you be any more of a family embarrassment?"

Lauren's face flushed sunrise red. She stomped back into the bathroom and spun the wheelchair to face her. Mother's head rocked back and forth with the momentum.

"I'm not the embarrassment! The problem with this trip isn't me. My situation, my whole damn life. and every problem in it, is about you. The constant denigration, the harping, the condemnation. I've had it!"

"That's what you call my helpful tips for you? Denigration? Let me tell you, disappointment that you have been, I can't imagine how you would have turned out without my guidance. You would be scrubbing the floors of some dropout husband, nursing his ignorant children. Everything you are, you owe to me. How am I repaid?" She slapped the side of her wheelchair. "You leave me crippled and disfigured."

Lauren shook with frustration. She snatched a lamp from the table and hurled it against the wall. It exploded into a hundred pieces with a thunderous crash.

"The accident wasn't my fault! But still, since then, I've tended to your every need. I bathe and dress you. I keep your skin moisturized. I take you to the garden each day. I arranged this trip to your favorite city—"

Three sharp knocks sounded at the door, this time with some force behind them.

"This is the police. Open the door."

Lauren bit her lip and hurried to the front door.

"You're on your own fixing this mess," Mother said.

"Open the door or I'll force it," the officer commanded.

Lauren opened the door a crack. The stout cop on the other side filled the doorway, a wall of blue with a silver badge and an intimidating peaked cap. He rammed his shoulder against the door. The chain snapped and Lauren reeled backwards.

"What's going on here?" the officer said, eyes drawn to the remnants of the shattered lamp.

"Nothing, everything is fine. We're just having a disagreement," Lauren snapped. She positioned herself between the cop and the bathroom doorway.

"Step outside with me ma'am, and we'll talk." The cop touched her elbow. Lauren yanked it away. She shoved the cop back with both hands.

"I'm not going anywhere. Leave us alone."

The cop moved at the speed of light. Before Lauren knew what hit her, she was face down on the carpet, hands pinned behind her. Her glasses flew across the room and the scene turned blurry. With two ratcheting clicks, the cold steel of handcuffs bit into her wrists.

"What the hell?" the cop said. "You're under arrest for assault." He yanked her to her feet and pushed her towards the door. "You can cool off downstairs in my car."

The words snuffed Lauren's anger in a flash. Dread welled up in its place, the feared, familiar black feeling. Like the empty sensation she had seeing her mother bleeding in the wreck. Like the dark abyss she wallowed into again three months later. The panic of separation filled her.

"No!" Lauren wailed. "No, I can't leave." Terror filled her voice. "My mother needs me. I have to care for her." She writhed in the cop's strong grip. Her voice gained a girl's high pitch. "I can't leave her alone here. Mother, tell him!"

Nothing but silence from the bathroom. The cop pushed Lauren into the hall.

"Mother, make him stop," she cried over her shoulder. "I'm sorry I yelled at you. I'll be good. I will. I have to take care of you."

The desk clerk stood in the hall, holding the elevator door open. The cop pushed Lauren inside.

"Thanks, officer," the clerk said. "I knew there would be trouble when she checked in."

◆◆◆

An hour later, detective Rick King stood in room 704. His tan overcoat was open, revealing a rumpled gray suit. The arresting officer briefed him.

"...so after she hit me, I had no choice but to restrain her. She was off the wall. I secured her in the car."

Detective King nodded and scribbled on a small pad.

"Her mother?" the cop asked.

Detective King stepped into the bathroom. He pulled the veil back from Mrs. Van Cleve's face. Deep burns covered her cheeks and forehead. Thick, black twine sutured both eyes shut with two crude Xs. More twine stitched across the woman's mouth in a makeshift, crosshatched smile. Tufts of dirty cotton protruded from her nostrils.

"Died a few months after a car accident paralyzed her," King said. "Looks like do-it-yourself taxidermy."

"Jeez, she must have really loved her mother," the cop said, face twisted in disgust.

The detective let the veil drop.

"Yeah, something like that."

Ω

Table for One

Vladimir "The Wolf" Rostovitch sat alone at the table in the dim restaurant. His two bodyguards stood at the entrance and redirected any potential customers to other establishments. Frank Molfetta, the owner, had invited The Wolf for a private supper.

The Wolf's shaved head gleamed in the single overhead light. Beneath his black jacket, the tips of crude tattoos poked out from his open white shirt. A gold wolf's head medallion hung from the matching chain at his thick neck. He leaned back in his chair and sipped a long-stemmed glass of red wine with the casual air of a king on his throne.

Frank shuffled in from the kitchen. He was a stout man with a shock of black hair only recently salted gray. Sadness etched his drawn face. A white apron, splotched dark brown from his kitchen work, encircled his waist. He carried a large salad.

"Your salad, Mr. Rostovitch," Frank said. He placed the bowl on the white table cloth. The Wolf nodded.

"Your business is empty," The Wolf commented. Years in New York hadn't thinned his thick Russian accent.

"First night open since the funeral," Frank said. "Just you here tonight, and I am the only staff, giving you and your dinner my full attention."

The Wolf pointed at Frank with a slosh of his wine glass. An errant drop stained the cloth with a red splash. "Wise move on your part. Rumor was you may have harbored me ill will."

"No, no," Frank said. A trace of fear crossed his face. "Just the opposite."

"My position," The Wolf sighed dramatically, "requires difficult decisions. But I am forced into them. People create intolerable situations."

Frank shifted his weight from one foot to the other. He averted his eyes.

"Now your son," The Wolf continued, "he created one of those intolerable situations." He stabbed a fork at his salad without looking. "At the club, at *my own* club, he treated my son Yuri with gross disrespect."

The Wolf's definition of disrespect was broad. Frank's son had stepped in when a drunken Yuri had torn off the blouse of a female patron. She had rebuffed the budding mobster's advances.

"You understand the position that puts me in," The Wolf said. "My son must be respected. He will take over the business someday."

Frank had planned the same for his son.

"The death of any young man is a tragedy," The Wolf said with a mouth full of lettuce. "It pained me to order it."

Frank looked at the floor. He softly repeated a Sicilian proverb his father had favored. "Family cannot go un-avenged."

The Wolf pointed his fork at Frank. "Precisely. And your acceptance of the situation is good for you." He waved his fork at the four walls. "Otherwise, business could suffer. Your fire insurance could lapse. Accidents happen."

Frank nodded and backed through the swinging kitchen door. The Wolf tore a chunk from a loaf of bread at his table. He ripped the piece in half with his teeth, gave it a few violent chews and swallowed.

Frank came back through the doors. A large white plate steamed and sizzled in his hands. The Wolf sniffed and smiled.

"You've prepared my favorite?" He pushed the salad away.

"Of course." Frank slid the plate before the Wolf. A sautéed steak filled the platter, garnished with onions and red peppers. "I hope it's to your liking."

"In Vladivostok," The Wolf reminisced, "we always ate what we hunted. It gave you the strength and the spirit of the beast it came from. Every real man has eaten Siberian tiger steak."

The Wolf chopped a section from the steak's corner and shoved it in his mouth. Frank held his breath in anticipation. The Wolf smiled, his black eyes alight.

"Excellent," he declared. "Better than usual."

"A special order," Frank offered. "A prime cut from a young bull."

The Wolf pounded his chest. "I feel stronger already!"

Frank nodded and turned for the kitchen. As he passed through the swinging doors, he shed the dour mask he'd been wearing and smiled. He rounded the empty steam table and stripped off his apron. He wadded it up in a ball and tossed it on the stone cold grill. He strode out the back door and into the night.

The pale, naked corpse of Yuri Rostovitch lay face down on the kitchen prep table, mouth gagged, hands bound underneath. Flaps of bloody skin lay like peeled onion skin from his back to his knees. A steak-sized chunk of flesh was missing.

◆◆◆

Seriously, you never wondered what really goes on in a restaurant's kitchen? You need to start.

Ω

Nora's Visitor

Nora Lovell bit her lower lip. The anticipation of her husband's return had her nervous as a cat.

Out her upper bedroom window, darkness enveloped the long approach to their Maine mansion. A cold north wind whipped the bare trees back and forth. At this time of year, everyone with good sense had already returned to civilization. Nora should have left the summer house and returned to the city weeks ago. But she decided to wait. Mr. Hiram Lovell's carriage would pull up at any moment, returning him from his steamship voyage and England. Then she and her husband would have the servants pack the house, and they would move back to the city. Together. Like a proper couple.

Nora turned up the wick on the oil lamp to throw light in the room's shadowy corners. How she wished this house had gas like their city home. Her husband clung to this place, just as three generations of his family had before him. Mr. Lovell would not hear of adding modern conveniences like a coal furnace and running water, despite her pleas that it was practically the twentieth-century.

Nora sat at her dressing table and reset a few hairpins to tighten her hair, piled high on her head. She straightened her tall collar and re-centered the ivory brooch at her throat. She thought she still looked quite good for forty. She kept her skin rosy and she still fit in her wedding dress. Mr. Lovell may travel a great deal on business, but she never feared he would stray. Every homecoming was a joyous reunion, where once again she felt complete.

Nora moved to the edge of her bed where she could see out the window and down the road. She had owned the ornately carved, four post masterpiece since her teens. Mr. Lovell had the rest of the furniture custom built to match the same shade of dark oak. Despite all the packing they would do this week, her bedroom set was the only furniture that would return to the city. Nora slept on no other bed.

The ticking clock marked each second's passage. She had the eerie sensation of waiting here before. Was that what her spiritualist circle called déjà vu? She shook the notion from her head. Of course this seemed familiar. How many days had she spent awaiting her husband's return? He had worn out carriage wheels to and from port this year.

A gust of wind elicited a soft moan from the house, a low chorus of flexing timbers and shifting window panes, like a collective cry against the approaching season of ice and snow. Mr. Lovell never paid it any mind, but Nora shared the servants' sentiments. It sounded too much like spirits. Nora shivered.

Being well after supper, the sound of the kitchen being cleaned for tomorrow's move should have echoed up the staircase. Nora could not hear a thing. If Bessie Mae thought she could wait for Mr. Lovell's return to start, and then delay their departure, she was most mistaken. Nora reached up and yanked the silk pull that rang the kitchen bell. Bessie had better get up here with a good explanation.

When she released the pull, another wave of familiarity swept over her. Not just the feel of the silk in her hand, but her uncharacteristic sharp feelings for lovely Bessie. She could almost forecast the next thing to happen, but then the premonition slipped away.

Oh silly woman, she thought. What nonsense. Déjà vu, indeed. It was the late hour. The waiting was confusing her.

A mix of anxiety and anticipation filled Nora as she watched the country lane beyond the house, praying for the flicker of her husband's carriage lanterns. Couldn't that driver hurry it up? She rubbed her hands together to burn some nervous energy.

The wind abated. She heard something. Soft, faint. A whisper?

No, she thought. A field mouse inside the plaster walls, perhaps. They scurry about at night. Or a raccoon made its way into the attic crawl space, his claws scratching on rafters. She had let the creaking of the house set her thinking of spirits, and now her mind was playing tricks on her.

The sound came again. There was no mistaking it. A human voice. Not a whisper really. It lacked that hushed confidential tone. It just sounded distant, like the person was at the far end of a long marble corridor. Unintelligible words faded in and out.

Bessie Mae, she thought. The cook was gossiping somewhere in the hall with the other servants. No wonder the kitchen isn't being cleaned. No wonder she hasn't answered my ring.

Nora opened the door and looked down the hallway. Empty.

"Bessie Mae!" No answer save another breeze-induced moan from the rafters. The hairs on her neck bristled. That same feeling of déjà vu crept over her again. She wanted to run down and give Bessie Mae a good lesson about ignoring her, but the silent empty staircase exuded an uncharacteristic foreboding. She knew she dared not leave her room, though could not say why. She slammed the door.

This was all too much. Why hadn't Mr. Lovell come home yet? The steamship was supposed to dock this morning. He should have been home by midday. If he was here, there would be no lollygagging by the servants. She would not be so confused and anxious. There would be a roaring fire, a sound night's sleep, and they would be on their way back to the bright vibrant city in the morning.

She resumed her sentinel position at the window. She could not help but worry. The road from the port was poorly maintained. The curve by the river, with that steep drop off, always made her cringe. Mr. Lovell might dismiss her fears, but carriages *had* overturned there. She pushed the thought from her mind.

The voice came again. This time it was no whisper. A male stranger's voice, clear as a bell.

"Are you here, Nora?"

Nora spun to face the room. The soft glow of the oil lamp showed it empty, but the voice sounded so close. A chill raced up her spine.

Her spiritualist circle had discussed this. A house this old would have the spirits of the dead in residence. The way Mr. Lovell's family was attached to the place, any who died here could still be trapped in the ether that surrounded the property. She kept her fear in check. The relatives would surely mean her no harm.

"Are you in this room?" the man said.

"Of course I'm in the room," she said, trying to stay calm. "Where are you?" She waited. An eternal minute passed without an answer. Pity welled within her for the tortured soul who could not move on.

"Who are you?" she called out. "Why do you haunt this place?"

More silence. The spirit had to be one of Mr. Lovell's relatives. Her husband should be here to witness this. Where could he be?

Nora picked the oil lamp up from her dressing table. With slow measured steps, she walked the perimeter of the room. She probed around the furniture and looked for any sign of the spirit's presence. Around the armoire, past the red stuffed leather chair, beside the tall dressers. Nothing was out of place.

As she rested the lamp on her night stand, a shape appeared in the stuffed chair. At first gray and indistinct, it darkened and morphed into a steadily more human form. Its faceless head swiveled around the room, searching. One hand reached out to Nora's bed.

This poor soul, she thought. Trapped between here and heaven's rewards. Alone and looking for reassurance.

She reached out. Her hand hovered over the dark figure's. Her heart skipped a beat as her fingers bent to caress its wrist. She brushed against it.

Her fingers burned hot as a blacksmith's forge.

In unison, she and the dark figure recoiled from each other. The spirit blinked out of existence. Nora checked her fingertips, certain they were seared. They glowed a warm red, but were undamaged.

Outside the clop and jangle of a carriage sounded at the front door. Nora leapt from the bed. Another premonition swept over her, this time dripping with dread. She looked out the window as a pair of harnessed black horses stopped in front of the mansion. Her heart dropped to her feet. It wasn't her husband's carriage. The steaming horses pulled an open wagon.

Nora's breath caught in her throat. She didn't recognize the man at the reins, but she knew the disheveled man at his side. It was Vincent, their driver. His arm was in a sling and his top hat was missing. Vincent was never to be outside without his hat. What could...

In the back of the wagon, a dark green tarp covered a shape that resembled only one thing. A human body.

"No, no, no," Nora said with a slow shake of her head. It's a workman from some farm, struck by accident by our carriage. Or a body they found as they traveled home. Something, anything but…

Vincent rose from the seat with great effort, as if he carried a burden far heavier than his own weight. He shuffled to the rear of the wagon and grabbed the canvas' edge.

Tears welled in Nora's eyes. Her lower lip trembled. "Please, God, no."

Vincent pulled back the canvas. Mr. Lovell lay stiff in the back of the truck, his face lifeless gray. His clothes were soaked and strands of algae clung to his coat.

"Lord, this can't be happening," she said. Her mind reeled. She turned hollow inside. Her strength, her purpose was gone. How could she face his sallow corpse? In a moment of madness, she thought that if she never went downstairs, time would roll backward and Mr. Lovell would still be alive.

◆◆◆

"Dude, it was so unreal." Kyle brushed his long blond hair away from his face.

"No way. You were really there?" Brantley said. He wore the same purple Theta Nu sweatshirt as Kyle. He refilled his glass from the pitcher of beer between them on the bar.

"Right there in the room," Kyle said. "Same haunted room everyone talks about at that old B&B. I was like, ready for a trip to the edge and that was the place for it. The place to plug into the beyond."

"I can't believe you went through with it, bro."

"And the room was like a total time capsule," Kyle said. "The bed, the chairs. No one ever changed it since she killed herself there."

"So you saw her?"

Kyle looked sheepish.

"Well, no. But like, I felt her. Like her presence was there. Like a force."

"Whoaaa, tell me about it, Luke Skywalker."

"Hey, dude," Kyle shot back. "She touched me. It was like instant frostbite."

"But you got no proof, no pictures."

"Oh, there's proof." Kyle nodded with satisfaction. "EVP."

"EVP?"

"Electronic Voice Phenomena. You don't hear the ghosts, but they record." Kyle pulled out an iPod and stuck the earbuds in his roommate's ears. "Listen up."

Brantley put his hands over the earbuds. He closed his eyes and concentrated, like a record producer ready to screen the next big hit.

"Listen. It's me, then her, then her again." Kyle pressed play.

Kyle's voice, hushed and tenuous, materialized in Brantley's head. A hint of fear warbled in his words.

"I'm here to help you tonight."

A pause, then a faint noise arose, a static-filled swoosh, well short of intelligible.

"Dude," Brantley said. "That's nothing."

Kyle slapped him on the back of the head.

"Shut up and listen."

Kyle's recorded voice came through the earbuds again.

"Are you here, Nora? Are you here in this room?"

Clear as polished diamonds, Nora spoke.

"Of course I'm in the room. Where are you?" A pause. Compassion tinged Nora's voice. "Who are you? Why do you haunt this place?"

"Dude," Brantley whispered, his eyes wide with amazement. "She thinks you're the ghost."

"I know. Isn't that wild?"

After viewing a Ghost Hunter's episode, I started to wonder how the world looks to poor spirit trapped here. Nora answered the question for me.

Ω

As Luck Would Have It

The black ball smacked around the spinning roulette wheel, jumping and dancing from number to number. The crowd's eyes followed the bouncing sphere as it ricocheted against the wheel's spokes in seeming defiance of the laws of physics.

On the gaming table's felt top, small collections of colored chips covered various numbers, but all were dwarfed by the red and gold tower on number twenty-four. For two straight spins, the house had added chips to the square, and to the earnings of Timmy Wayne.

Tension knit the crowd into a mass of anticipation. Hands clasped and wrung, eyes darted around the table, hearts raced. Timmy stood at ease, battered cowboy hat tipped back on his head, white silk shirt untucked and unbuttoned halfway down his long, lean chest. His brown eyes watched the wheel with only casual interest.

The black ball bounced and smacked and stopped. The wheel coasted down. The croupier called the result.

"Twenty-four! The gentleman wins again."

A cheer went up from the little crowd. The croupier cleared the losing bets from the table. He counted out a stack of Timmy's latest winnings. As he went to slide them to number twenty-four, a hand reached out and tapped back his wrist.

The pit boss wore a dark suit with a bright red tie and a gold nameplate on his breast pocket. "Mr. Wayne will be cashing out."

The look on Timmy's face was more of resignation than surprise. Two muscular bouncers stepped up on either side of him. He raised his hands palms up and stepped back from the table. The croupier scooped Timmy's winnings into a plastic container and handed it to the pit boss. The pit boss led Timmy and the hired help to the cashier's cage.

"Can't cheat at roulette," Timmy said. "At least a player can't."

"I didn't say you were, Timmy," the pit boss said. "I never do. The Vapor Trail just doesn't like your luck."

The cashier handed Timmy back a banded stack of bills. He tucked them in the side pocket of his black cargo pants.

"How can I make a living if you don't let me work?" Timmy said.

"Make a living down at the MGM Grand," the pit boss said.

He jerked a thumb at the exit door, and the beefcakes escorted Timmy out. The desert heat hit like a hammer when they passed from the air conditioned lobby to the teeming masses outside. Timmy passed bouncer a twenty when they reached the sidewalk.

"Thanks for being gentle," he said.

"You get what you give," one of the bouncers said.

Timmy walked south along the Strip. The setting sun touched the mountains to the west. Las Vegas' neon frenzy was about to blast into high gear. He could hit the MGM, the Aladdin, or at any of the big casinos. But the few thousand in his pocket would cover this week's expenses. Other gamblers would have had to keep going, determined to ride the hot streak until it burned out. Timmy had no such pressure. His hot streak never cooled.

The last five years in Vegas, things had consistently broken his way. In a town where nearly everyone went home a loser, he always went home a winner. He didn't win every hand he played, or hit the jackpot on every spin of a slot machine, but by evening's end, he always came out ahead. Always. The sliver of a percent advantage the house was always supposed to have, seemed to default to Timmy. The longer he played, the larger his winnings.

He soon had a rep among the casinos as a man to be watched. Accused of counting cards, the big houses banned him from blackjack and poker. All he could play were slots, roulette and a few other games of pure luck. Once in a while, a casino bounced him out like the Vapor Trail just had, but usually he just won small amounts and walked away. He'd just joked about making a living gambling with the pit boss, but he actually did. A nice, low profile, middle class living.

So with his bills covered tonight, there was no need to be greedy. He returned to his car, a four-year-old BMW he'd treated himself to before he realized he needed to be more discreet about his gift. He just couldn't part with it.

He fired up the big straight six and wheeled the car out to the Strip. He gunned the engine and the tach screamed to the redline. The car launched like a rocket.

He pulled his foot off the gas pedal. The engine continued a full force growl. The car kept accelerating. He pounded the gas pedal a few times to unstick the throttle cable. No change.

Up ahead, the stop light blazed red. A sea of red taillights stared at him upstream of the crosswalk.

He jammed both feet on the brake pedal. It sank to the floor. The car upshifted into third. The stopped traffic came up fast, brake lights glowing with a warning he could not heed.

He held the steering wheel in a death grip. He glanced right and left, but the gaudy strip had him hemmed in with oncoming traffic on one side and a throng of pedestrians on the other.

The stop light turned green. The cars pulled away in a pack. He was on their tail in a second.

The car in the center lane shifted one lane to the left and opened a hole. Timmy yanked the wheel left and aimed. The BMW screamed between the other two lanes of cars. It cleared their door handles by inches. Ahead, the Strip stretched uncharacteristically empty for at least a mile. The BMW's speedometer passed seventy.

Ahead on the right, workers had imploded the old Sundancer casino. A sagging, flimsy chain link fence ran along the edge of the sidewalk, and behind it rose an enormous pile of excavated sand. Timmy spun the wheel right and leaned on his horn.

Startled pedestrians looked up and scattered. The BMW hopped the curb at eighty-five and slammed into the fence. The fence pulled from its support posts with a machinegun-like pinging of the attaching wires. The BMW slowed. Then it rammed the sand pile head-on. The nose buried itself halfway to the windshield. Airbags deployed with an explosive whoosh and caught Timmy like a pillow catching a maid's tossed chocolate mint.

Hours later, the paramedics had certified him unharmed, but a tow truck had his car loaded for a trip to automotive intensive care. The driver surveyed the scene and said, "Man, you sure are lucky."

When the taxi dropped him off at his suburban ranch house, the neighborhood was dark. No houselights. No streetlights. He opened his door and a rush of hot air rolled over him like he'd opened an oven. The air conditioning had been down for hours. He entered his home and flipped the living room light switch to no effect.

"Wonderful," he sighed.

He was tired, and sore and hungry. Visions of a refrigerator full of rotting food popped into his head. Sleeping in this heat was going to be impossible. Maybe the usually cooler basement would be livable. He felt his way to the kitchen, found the flashlight under the sink and was relieved when it snapped on. At least one thing was going right.

When he opened the door to the basement, the smell of rotten eggs engulfed him. His pulse doubled. A gas leak, probably from the water heater, maybe the dryer. He wasn't about to find out which. The house was one spark away from being a bomb. He ran out the front door and down to the street. With the last few volts of his cell phone's power, he called 911 for the second time that day.

It was after midnight when the Southwest Gas technicians finished airing out his house and declared it safe. The gas line to the dryer had split during the day. Thirty minutes later, NV Power had the neighborhood's electricity humming again. A squirrel had found its way into a transformer early that evening.

"Good thing your power was out," the SW Gas tech had said. "One spark from flipping on a light switch and your house here would have been one smoking hole in the ground."

The bad luck that had spoiled his milk also saved his life.

◆◆◆

After that kind of day, Timmy slept in the next morning. He rolled over to avoid the desert daylight streaming in between the slats of his blinds. Through his bleary eyes he made out the dark mass of a man sitting in the chair by his bed. He bolted upright, wide awake.

"Jesus, I thought you'd never wake up," the man said.

He sat hunched in the chair, legs spread apart, elbows on his knees. He wore a faded yellow T-shirt from some casino giveaway. The hems of his shorts were frayed into cilia. A red, ropy scar ran down the side of his sunburned neck and under his shirt, only to exit down his right arm. A sun-damaged, tangled mess of hair pointed in multiple directions. The stubble on his chin and cheeks shimmered with premature gray.

But two more important items grabbed Timmy's attention. The wide, wild look in the man's darting eyes, and the coal black .45 he fingered between his knees.

"Who are you? What do you want?" Timmy said. His mouth went dry.

"Name's Harlan Bidwell," the man said. He waved a lazy salute with the big handgun. "Pleased to meet ya. What do I want? To make things even."

"Harlan, y-you must have me confused with someone else. I-I don't know you."

"Ah, but I knows you, Timothy R. Wayne, same way all the pit bosses knows you. You're the man with all the luck, the man who just can't lose."

Dread landed in Timmy's gut like a mortar round. He'd always been afraid of someone taking him as a high roller, and thinking he'd be an easy target.

"It's really not like that. Look around, you can see I'm not rich. But there's two grand in my pants there, a few hundred more in a box in the hall closet. Take it all, the plasma TV, whatever you want."

"Don't want to steal nothing," Harlan said. "Told you, I want to make things even."

He smiled like a viper. His eyes bounced around in their sockets. He looked 100% whacked. Timmy realized he was in deep trouble.

"I don't understand," he said.

"Don't ya never wonder about all your luck, all your good fortune? For every ten men that goes into a casino, five leaves winners and five leaves losers. Thems the odds. But it ain't true when you join the crowd. You always win. That means for the other ten, one more's gotta be an extra loser. Stands to reason or the whole applecart gets upset. Do the math, Einstein."

Timmy slid back a few inches on his bed. He searched his memory for something, anything, nearby he could use as a weapon.

"But we ain't just talking casinos, here," Harlan continued. "We're talking life. You just wander around attracting good luck like tuna attracts cats. All that luck's gotta come from somewhere. Know where that is?"

Timmy shook his head. Harlan tapped his own chest with the side of the gun barrel.

"Comes from me, that's where. Leaves me with parents dead of cancer, a fiancée who inherits big time and runs off, a house swallowed by a sinkhole, and more accidents than a Hollywood stuntman. Anything good that coulda happened to me..." He touched the gun barrel to his breastbone. "...done happened to you."

He pointed the gun toward Timmy's head. Timmy looked straight down the dark barrel and into eternity.

"It doesn't work that way," Timmy pleaded. "But take everything here. Please. Make it even."

"That ain't gonna make it even. Luck's still gonna run downhill to you, lessen you stop breathin'. And damned if I didn't do my best to make it look like an accident. Jacked up your car. Slit up the gas lines. Even poisoned your damn food as a backup, but the power outage spoilt it. But your goddamn luck kept workin' overtime. So now it's down to this."

His eyes sparkled with madness. He cocked the pistol's hammer. Timmy's jaw dropped. Sweat rolled down his forehead.

"'Bout a foot 'tween this bullet and your brain," Harlan said. "Your luck has finally done run out."

He pulled the trigger and the .45 roared.

◆◆◆

An hour later, flashing blue police lights lit Timmy's house like a carnival ride. Inside, a cop peered past Timmy and into his bedroom across the yellow crime scene tape. On the other side, the head of the man sprawled on the floor looked like a shattered watermelon. The cop gritted his teeth and turned back to Timmy.

"Unbelievable," he whispered.

"I was sure I was dead," Timmy said. "But when he pulled the trigger, the back half of the gun just exploded in his face."

The cop smiled and clapped him on the shoulder. "Tell you what, you must be one lucky guy."

◆◆◆

On a trip to Las Vegas, I watched someone win a pretty big pot of cash, and looked at all the people around him who lost. I started thinking about the laws of probability and this story came out in a rush.

Me? I sat down and dropped a dollar in the penny slots. Fifteen minutes later I was up to $1.25. Losses soon dropped it back to $1.01. I cashed out, determined to leave Vegas a winner.

Ω

Man's Best Friend

Carlton entered the butcher shop off 23rd Street. Varying cuts of freshly sliced meat, a pastiche in pinks and white, lay displayed in a long, curved-glass counter. Harvey the butcher looked up from behind. His white apron had the usual assortment of red and brown splotches earned through a day's honest work.

"Dr. Tressler," Harvey said, with the smile he reserved for his most prized customers. "I have a line on something special for you."

Carlton Tressler wished Harvey's rare finds really were for him. But most of what Carlton's butcher shop purchases didn't go to feed him, or his wife, Holly.

"Zebra," Harvey said, like he'd announced the discovery of an eighth continent. "Completely legit, farm-raised in South Africa."

"Hate to burst your bubble," Carlton said, "but we tried zebra about two years ago."

Harvey looked disappointed, then confused. "Really?"

"Yep. In between gazelle and wildebeest."

Which was before kangaroo, and after yak. The Tressler household had cycled through an untold variety of creatures trying to feed their dog, Juke. Holly Tressler had mastered cooking meats few knew available.

"Well," Harvey said, "if it was two years ago…maybe we could give zebra another try."

"Nope," Carlton said. "Once Juke starts reacting, we can never go back."

The veterinarian had characterized it as an extreme allergic reaction. Juke could eat a type of meat for a while, then his immune system created an antibody against it. Then they had to switch Juke to a different shrink-wrapped prey.

The dog's allergic reaction didn't manifest as a case of the sniffles. It was closer to road rage. With each passing day on a specific meat, Juke would eventually get more and more aggressive, and not just to strangers. Carlton and Holly had the scars to prove that.

"Today, I'll take a half-pound of flank steak for Holly and me," Carlton said.

"And Juke?"

"Holly's getting him something."

"You're good owners," Harvey said with admiration. "There's nothing you don't sacrifice for your pet."

◆◆◆

Carlton tucked the steaks under one arm as he walked the last few blocks to his brownstone townhouse. As he ticked off each memorized slab of concrete sidewalk, the tension in his neck grew. With each step, his inhalations grew shorter and sharper, and he concentrated to keep his heart rate at bay. By the time he reached the front stoop, prickles of sweat sprinkled his upper lip. He wiped them away and took the steps one at a time. He braced himself and opened the front door.

The hallway was quiet. He stepped inside, and silently pressed the door closed like it was made of crystal. The omnipresent acrid scent of dog urine drifted by him, and he subconsciously filtered it out. Deep, white scars gouged the dark paneling along the lower half of the walls. A shredded chew bone lay in the middle of the mashed hall carpet.

Not the recommended first impression to give visitors, but visitors were a thing of the past at the Tressler house. On his best day, Juke still put up an active defense against intruders, and even invited guests were intruders.

Carlton knew Juke and Holly were home somewhere. Juke's oversized, black leather muzzle hung on its post on the wall. Juke looked like Hannibal Lecter when he wore it during his infrequent forays into the outside world. But the Tresslers knew better than to take him out without it. After what happened to that poodle years ago...

At the end of the hallway, two shining, narrowed eyes appeared in the shadows. An inch at a time, Juke emerged from out of the darkness. First a broad, black snout, next a set of bared, glistening white teeth, then atop his massive head, a pair of ragged ears, swept back and ready for combat. His powerful pit bull shoulders crossed into the daylight. The ebony dog moved as if being born of the shadow, pulling a part of the darkness with it. Juke swung his head and let out a low, rumbling growl.

Juke stopped and blocked the hall entrance to the kitchen. Carlton slid left into the living room and then through the other kitchen doorway. All the doorways to the kitchen were open, the doors long ago splintered by repeated canine impact.

Holly sat hunched over the kitchen table, two legs of which sported silver bands of duct tape repairs. Her large glasses had slid down a bit on her nose as she read today's newspaper. She looked up across them at Carlton. Dark circles puffed beneath her eyes. Her hair seemed a shade grayer, an impression Carlton attributed to the light.

Carlton entered the kitchen and put the steaks on the chipped, yellowed countertop. On the floor to the right sat the large freezer box. They'd purchased it to save a few dollars buying exotic meats in bulk.

By the time he'd turned back to the table, Juke had stuck his head in from the hallway. It brushed level against the door jamb's cobwebbed striker. Juke snorted.

"How are you, Holly-day?" Carlton asked his wife. He hadn't called her that in years. It sounded forced.

Holly shot a sidelong glance at Juke. "The same as usual."

Carlton did a quick calculation and realized it had been three years of *the usual*. Juke hadn't been home from the shelter two weeks before his true personality manifested. A battalion of doctors, a long list of failed medications and a small fortune passed by before the diagnosis settled on food allergies. As a cute, damaged puppy, they could not bring themselves to return him to face certain death as unadoptable. As a brutal, angry dog, they did not dare try.

Not that they would consider it. They'd suffered enough loss. After their sons' murder/suicide pact, the empty house screamed their guilt each day, Juke was to fill that void and bring them out of the darkness. If they couldn't even raise a dog...

"Well, I brought us home steaks," Carlton said. He meant the statement to be triumphant, but somehow it sounded quite sad.

◆◆◆

Carlton and Holly cooked together, the way they had when they were newlyweds, she the meat and he the vegetables. He lit a single candle at the bare table's center. They ate in silence, never out of Juke's watchful glare. At the end, Carlton cleared the table as Holly stared off at nothing. Juke let out a growl and a yip.

"He's been waiting to eat," Holly said. "I need to feed him."

"You know we don't need to do it this way," Carlton said. "We can get someone else to feed him. This is a big city."

"He's my dog," Holly said. "I picked him out. He's my responsibility." She sighed. "I'll feed him."

♦♦♦

Carlton rose early the next day and tiptoed through his morning routine, lest he awaken the sleeping. He crept downstairs from the bedroom. At the bottom, he froze as he saw Juke in the hallway, already awake. Time for the test, to see how last night's dinner settled with the dog. If Juke was already allergic, it would be a race for the front door.

Juke approached Carlton. He wagged his stubby tail and licked Carlton's hand. He'd never done either before.

Another time, any other time, all Carlton would have felt was relief. But his joy was tempered by last night's memories of what they had gone through for Juke.

Juke followed Carlton into the kitchen. A spray of blood droplets on the floor had escaped Carlton's late night cleanup. He popped open the lid of the freezer.

Inside, frost coated Holly's hair and fogged her glasses. Her right forearm was missing.

♦♦♦

Every day, I see people going to great lengths for their pets; standing in the rain so a dog can relieve itself, planning vacations around getting a pet sitter, buying toys and even pet furniture. I wondered what the most extreme example of that might turn into. Of course, it got creepy.

Ω

The Gift

The bull water buffalo came out of nowhere, just materialized in the glare of the rising sun. Kayla Jefferson stood on the Land Rover's brakes, and prayed. The wheels locked. The Rover skidded sideways, and kicked a plume of dirt and rocks in its wake. It lurched to a stop inches from the enormous beast. Kayla's pulse thundered in her ears.

The animal stared an impassive look through the driver's door window, its face so close that each breath fogged a circle on glass. Huge black horns protruded from its head, each ending in a sharp, shiny taper.

Kayla's iron grip on the wheel tightened further as she looked into the brown eyes locked on hers. A buffalo could make short work of a Rover.

The bull gave Kayla a huffing snort, a derisive assertion of its superiority. Then its head swung away, it ambled off the road, and into the savannah. Kayla exhaled the breath she hadn't realized she was holding. She reined in her racing heartbeat, and drove on. Her Atlanta commutes had been lousy, but at least there were no water buffaloes.

Her drive from the city each day to the rural township school took her through a lovely stretch of South African countryside. This October, the southern hemisphere spring, the landscape was awash in dark greens and new flowers. The invigorating, sweet fresh scent soon washed away the fear from the buffalo encounter. It felt good to see optimistic green shoots encroach on the country's pervasive poverty.

Outside the township, the Range Rover closed on Mbele's food stand. Built from scrap wood and tin, it was the place to shop for fresh fruit and vegetables. Mbele puttered outside the stand, arranging bananas and cassavas. The African sun had wrinkled his jet black skin beyond his years. Scattered gray speckled his short wiry hair. He wore a loose, faded red polo shirt over tan shorts and sandals. His face broke into a broad gap-toothed grin as the Rover pulled in for their shared favorite morning ritual.

"Kayla, dear," he said. "A welcome sight as always."

She couldn't help but smile as she got out of the car. The long print wrap she wore made her look even taller than her 5'9" frame. She'd bought it in the city when she first arrived. It was black with a yellow and orange diamond pattern, light, comfortable, and very African. The last attribute had been the selling point.

Since graduating from Morehouse University, she felt the need to explore the "African" in her African-American heritage. Her friends landed high-paying Fortune 50 jobs. She followed her heart, and signed up to teach a year of South African elementary school at a fraction of her friends' starting salaries. While they house hunted in New York and Chicago, she ordered mosquito netting from an outdoorsman website. Almost everyone roundly ridiculed her decision.

"Jambo, Mbele. It's another beautiful day," she said to the food stand owner.

"Are the students mastering their studies?" he replied.

Kayla got a kick out of the British syntax even the poorest citizen used.

"They are, for sure," she replied. "All wonderful children."

"The children love you. Your family must be proud."

They were. Especially her idolized father, a high school teacher. His example influenced her decision to teach. Confined to a wheelchair by the long-term effects of high blood pressure, there was no chance that he would see what she was accomplishing during her year in the village. She sent megabytes of pictures and video, but she wished he could see her teach, see her do what she did best.

"What looks good, Mbele?" she asked.

"Bananas today," Mbele said, tapping a bunch with a long thin stick. "Fresh this morning from the tree. None better for miles."

This was no sales pitch. If Mbele said these were the best, they were. He was a legend in the village for finding the best fresh produce, even during droughts. Kayla dismissed the rumors of witchcraft that swirled around the kind man. Superstition flourished on every continent.

"Very well," she said. "Give me six." These would be rewards for her children today. Best speller. Best in long division.

Best behaved. The fruit some American children avoided was a tremendous incentive to undernourished South Africans.

Mbele took his time inspecting a bunch of bananas. "Rumors are that you broke up a fight last week."

"Does all the news pass through your shop?" Kayla said. "Yes, there was a little fight."

"Five-on-one is not so little, especially five much older boys."

Five high school boys, some bigger than Kayla, had cornered Joseph, one of her boys, after school. She intervened and saved her student from a beating.

"You shamed the five," Mbele continued, "for picking on the weak. You smothered violence with words."

"One of my father's lessons he taught me about teaching. In twenty-five years, he said he diffused many fights, participated in none."

"You had a wise father."

"His support gave me the courage to come here. You know, I don't even know what sparked the fight."

"Tribal nonsense," Mbele said. "Without Afrikaners to fight, some think we must fight each other. Joseph is my cousin's son. You have my family's thanks, and mine."

Mbele tore six bananas from the bunch and handed them to Kayla. She put some coins on the counter. He swept the coins into a metal box. He pulled something from the box and closed his fist over it.

Kayla reached for the bananas. Mbele grabbed her right wrist. His calloused hands had a powerful grip for so slight a man. He rolled her wrist until her open palm faced up. He dropped the object from the box into her hand.

A glossy tooth glistened in her palm. It looked like the canine from a small carnivore, a few inches long and white as bleached salt. A small hole bored in the root readied it to thread on a necklace.

Last spring, if someone had put an animal part in her hand, she would have screamed and dropped it like it was on fire. Africa had changed all that. Animal fur and bones were respected here, sometimes revered, for reputed magical powers.

She gave Mbele a quizzical look.

"A gift for you," he said.

"What's it for?" Kayla asked.

Mbele laughed.

"Miss Kayla! It is a child's trinket. Have you started believing silly tales of magic?"

"Oh, no," Kayla said, her face blushing.

"Of course," Mbele said. "Now the superstitious sometimes say a hyena tooth is a spirit catcher, a magnet for traveling souls as they pass to the afterlife."

Kayla's eyebrows arched.

"Really?"

Mbele laughed even deeper.

"Come, Miss Kayla. Who can put stock in such things? It is just a bauble for you. A souvenir."

Kayla buried the tooth in the pocket of her dress, embarrassed again by her gullibility.

"Thank you," she said. She grabbed her bananas. "I'll see you tomorrow."

"Yes, tomorrow," said Mbele. His eyes twinkled. "I will see you tomorrow."

◆◆◆

Kayla's school was a humble, unpainted block structure at the intersection of two dirt streets in the shabby village. Six small classrooms subdivided the building. A relief organization had built it right after the end of apartheid to ensure there was a place for this first generation of free black children to go to school. Large windows in each room let in light and any passing breeze, compensating for the lack of electricity. The missing outside door left an open threshold that provided cross ventilation.

In Kayla's classroom, twenty small desks with twenty small chairs faced her desk at the head of the class. Blackboards covered two walls. Artwork papered the third, crayon masterpieces drawn by her second graders with the theme of "My Happiest Day." Yellow suns, green grass and smiling stick figures abounded. The tech-free classroom would appall American parents. Kayla reveled in the refreshing simplicity.

Here, she *taught*. No crutches, no diversions, no backup. It was just her, her chalkboard and twenty students with twenty pencils. Every moment created a personal connection with an eager young mind. Every day brought the reward of seeing children experience the epiphany of academic understanding. Minimalism distilled learning to its pure core, as her father always said it was supposed to be.

Kayla arrived and sat at her desk. She set the six bananas at the far corner. The children would see the prize even before they knew the rules to win it, then beg to know today's game. Bananas were always a favorite.

The children filtered in. The room filled with a sea of blue and white uniform shirts. The usual buzz and shriek of children's conversation filled the air. Kayla was just opening the class science book when she heard Joseph cry out from the doorway.

"Miss Jefferson! Come quick. It's a dog! A big dog!"

Kayla kicked her chair back against the wall and flew to the doorway. The potential threat to her children sent her heart racing.

She pulled Joseph behind her and stood in the doorway. Several yards away sat a jet black Siberian Husky. A touch of gray speckled its muzzle. Its sharp white teeth sparkled in the morning sun. Kayla had seen many dogs in South Africa, but almost all were undernourished, yellow bone bags of indistinct pedigree. Never a dog like this.

The dog barked like a shotgun blast. It whipped its muzzle through the air in a circle, like a man dropping a race's green starting flag. Teeth bared, it burst for the doorway at a run.

Kayla went on full alert. She pushed Joseph back into the classroom. She grabbed the closest thing at hand, one of the children's chairs. She pointed the feet at the onrushing dog like some imitation lion tamer, and braced for the assault.

The dog skidded to a stop three feet away. It sat back on its haunches, and cocked its head at Kayla. Its tongue lolled out of its mouth and it began to pant. The edges of its lips curled up, and Kayla swore the Husky smiled.

The dog dropped on its side with a thud, raising a small cloud of dust. Then it rolled on its back, all four paws in the air and whimpered a request for a belly rub.

Kayla sighed with relief. Perhaps she'd misinterpreted enthusiasm for aggression.

"What are you doing, boy?" she said. She planted the chair on the ground, stepped forward and knelt by the dog. She gave the silky fur of its belly a healthy rub and the dog shuddered with delight. A calm, centered feeling came over her as she stroked the dog.

"You're not dangerous, are you, boy?" she whispered. The dog closed its eyes in satisfaction. "What home have you wandered away from?"

Kayla heard some snickers from behind her. She turned and a swarm of small black heads jockeyed for position in the classroom window, confused to not see mortal combat.

"What are you all doing?" she snapped. "Everyone back to their seats!"

Panicked eyes went wide. The voyeurs disappeared from the window frame. The air filled with the scrape of tiny seats against the bare concrete floor. Kayla gave the dog two solid thumps to its belly.

"Go home, boy," she said. "I have to teach."

She returned to the classroom The dog just lay on the ground, smiled and watched her leave.

"Good morning students!" she sang on her way to the front of the classroom.

"Good morning, Miss Jefferson!" they sang in return. Then the class broke into their morning song:

> *"Wake up early with the rising sun,*
> *To learn at school and have some fun.*
> *Strong and proud of who we are,*
> *Each of us can be a star."*

As if on cue, a scratching noise came from the doorway, followed by a soft mournful whimper. The Husky's nose appeared in the threshold. Joseph was up from his seat and had his head out the window in an instant.

"Miss Jefferson! It's the dog. He wants to come in."

Kayla slapped her desk twice.

"Joseph, take your seat. I am not letting some strange dog in the classroom."

A muted whimper sounded outside the door and triggered a collective whine from the students.

"C'mon Miss Jefferson."

"You said he was a good dog."

"Just let him see inside."

Her resolve wavered. The class had been doing so well all week. They really all deserved bananas today. She went to the doorway. The docile dog lay on the stoop, and stared up at her with pleading eyes. It squeaked an entry request.

"Can you behave?" Kayla asked the dog.

The dog rolled on its side and rotated two paws straight up in the air.

"All right," Kayla said. She waved the dog forward. The Husky rolled to its feet and trotted in. It stopped at Kayla's feet and licked her hand. She scratched his head and felt that comforting warmth again.

Kayla smiled and returned to her desk. The dog followed an obedient two paces behind, and then made a solo lap around the classroom. The dog looked right and left, soaking in the sights, sounds and smells of the classroom. Excited little hands reached out and stroked his soft coat as he passed and the classroom was awash in appreciative oohs and ahhs. The dog even rewarded the brave few who caressed his muzzle with a lick of the fingertips. He took position back at the doorway, rested back on its haunches, and panted happily. The children's excited dialogue reached a crescendo.

"All right! All right!" Kayla said in her firm-teacher-voice. "Let's do our work or the friendly dog goes back outside. I want your science books on your desk and your eyes up here."

Books hit desktops with staccato thumps and the room went silent.

"We are on page sixty," Kayla said, scanning the students' books to make sure they were on the right page. She shot a quick glance at the dog, panting and attentive in the corner. He already understood the rules. Assured he was no threat to classroom order, she started to teach.

Kayla went through the lesson with fluid ease. She drew her students into the material, tailoring questions to the personal strengths and weaknesses she had discerned over the months. She shot an occasional penetrating glance at Joseph, arresting his mischief before he even fully visualized it. Like a border collie herding sheep, she kept the students together, bringing strays back to the fold, moving them towards understanding.

After thirty minutes, the dog rose and trotted to Kayla at the front of the room. He gave her hand a warm lick. She looked down in the dog's deep brown eyes. The dog gave a happy "yip" and loped out the door.

The children rose in an excited mass and crammed the window for a glimpse of the retreating Husky. Kayla looked over their heads in time to see the canine vanish between buildings down the street.

"Show's over," she said, clapping her hands over her head. "Everyone back in their seats."

As the children took their places, she looked again at the empty street. Somehow, she knew that would be the dog's only visit.

◆◆◆

That afternoon, as soon as she was in range of the city's cell towers, her phone rang. She pulled over and answered

"Kayla?"

"Mom!" she answered. "What a surprise. You would not believe what happened today—"

"Honey," Kayla's mother cut her off, "I have bad news."

Kayla's heart sank.

"Your father passed away last night."

Kayla's body went numb, her stomach dropped to the ground. "How…"

"His heart, Honey. He was just resting, watching television after dinner. He fell asleep and was gone. He didn't feel a thing."

"Oh, Mom," Kayla said.

"He talked about you at dinner. He wanted to see you teaching so badly. He was so proud of you…." Sobs choked off the rest of what she had to say.

"Mom, I'll get a flight home. I'll call you right back, O.K.?"

There were some muffled sounds of assent from nine thousand miles away, then a clear "I love you."

"I love you, too, Mom." The line went silent.

Something twitched in her pocket. She reached in and pulled out Mbele's gift, the hyena's tooth. She closed her hand around it. The same affectionate reassurance she felt petting the dog at school warmed her palm. The sight of the dog's soft, expressive eyes flashed before her.

A spirit catcher, Mbele had told her.

The dog. Her father.

A gift for you, Mbele had said.

She wrapped both hands around the tooth, closed her eyes, and wept for joy.

♦♦♦

I believe that every soul has the chance to make one goodbye on the way to what awaits us next. Not every soul takes advantage of it, just those with a strong connection who didn't get to say goodbye. I had the gift of experiencing it once, before I even knew the person had passed on. I hope someday it happens to you.

Ω

Down on the Farm

Mike Cavendish snapped wide awake. Heavy pounding rattled his door on its hinges. He shook his head. A post-midnight summons made no sense. As a USAID advisor helping Honduran farmers, his skills weren't in demand around the clock.

He sat up and swung his bare feet onto the concrete floor. He hated being awake so early. Only in the wee morning hours did the temperature and humidity retreat to bearable and make this the prime time for sleep.

The rapid fire hammering at his door resumed.

"I'm coming," he yelled as he passed from his bedroom to the main room, clad in exercise shorts and a T-shirt. His utilitarian house was impressive by Central American standards. The three rooms gave him the space to live and conduct business. He reveled in the simplicity of life here compared to the regimented quarter century he'd spent in the Army.

He opened his front door. The violent banging was out of proportion with the little girl on the porch, a familiar ten-year-old with waist-length straight black hair. She wore a faded red jumper over a white blouse. Her feet were bare. She panted like she'd run a marathon.

"Maria?" Mike said. He squinted into the darkness up the dirt road. "Where is your mother?"

"*Venga me, Señor C,*" she said gesturing like a windmill for him to follow her. "Come to our house. Mama needs you. *Ricardo esta en la casa. Tanto terrible.*" She grabbed Mike's hand and tried to drag him out the door.

Maria's mother Elena was Mike's housekeeper. He didn't need one, but she needed work to support her three kids, and it didn't cost much to have her. Twice a week, she cleaned up and did his laundry. Elena was friendly, and he thought she trusted him. Sending Maria here proved him right.

"Relax, Maria," he said. "I'll come with you. *Puedo ayudar le.*" He took one step out the door. That was all the commitment Maria needed. She dropped his hand and bolted down the street to her house. Mike jogged after her. At fifty-two, he wasn't going to keep up. He was still fit, but a career on active duty left a legacy of long-term damage.

Maria stopped in front of her house and gestured for him to hurry up.

"*¡Rapido, Señor C!*" she said, and ducked inside.

The ramshackle house in the village had been quite crowded when Elena's sons, Ricardo, eighteen, and Ramon, sixteen, had still lived there. Months ago, the two inseparable boys left to find work in one of the larger towns. Maria said Ricardo returned. Under only the most dire of circumstances would Ricardo have returned without Ramon.

Elena met Mike at the door. She was short, with olive skin and the deeply creased features earned by a lifetime working outdoors. She wore a long housedress. She made the sign of the cross.

"*Gracias, Señor C,*" she said. Her voice cracked with emotion. "You must help. Ricardo, he come home tonight. He very sick. *Venga.*"

On the kitchen table, Ricardo lay on his stomach. He was naked and his arms and feet hung off the table into space. A towel lay draped across his butt for modesty, but it did not hide the massive damage his body sustained. His feet and legs were torn and blistered, as if he had been running through the jungle barefoot. His pale, drawn face appeared wasted from the inside. Two bloodshot eyes stared out through half closed lids.

But the worst sight was his back. The skin, torn open in many long strips, revealed red, tender muscle. Some deeper lacerations exposed bone. A patchwork of both fresh and dried blood covered the space between the jagged tears. Maggots wiggled in the grayer portions at the wounds edges. That told Mike that some of these injuries were days old. In his years of combat service, he had never seen anything like this.

Mike's heart sank. Ricardo was a gentle, compassionate boy with big dreams. Mike flashed back to the young soldiers he watched die in Iraq and Afghanistan. His medical training kicked in and he went to work.

Mike took Ricardo's pulse. Its slow rhythm was faint as a feather's caress. Each shallow breath took Herculean effort.

Between exposure, blood loss and shock, Ricardo was lucky to be alive.

"Maria," Mike said, "I need some water. *Agua mas caliente*. And I need some clean cloth for bandages."

Maria dashed off to the kitchen. Elena sat beside the table with Ricardo's unresponsive hand cupped in hers. She squeezed it and tears welled in her eyes. She softly prayed the Hail Mary.

"Elena," Mike said, "where did Ricardo and Ramon go?"

"They look for work all over," Elena said. Her eyes never left Ricardo. "A little here, a little there. They say that they go to work at the Montedolores Plantation. Then I no hear from them for months, until Ricardo arrive tonight."

"Did he say anything to you?" Mike asked.

"*No habla nada*," Elena said, sniffing back her tears. "He just collapse in the house. You save my boy."

Helping Ricardo would be tough. The wounds on the weakened boy's back were deep and infected. On a battlefield, Ricardo would have gotten antibiotics and been airlifted to a hospital. Here, Mike had nothing but hot water and his meager skills.

Maria returned with a steaming pan of hot water. She laid it on the chair by the table. She had two white sheets and a towel slung over her shoulder. She handed them to Mike.

He dipped the towel in the water. He wrung it out and swabbed around Ricardo's wounds, cleaning the blood and dirt from his skin. Mike looked down at Ricardo's immobile face and thanked God the boy couldn't feel a thing.

"Elena," Mike said. "We really need a doctor here. Ricardo is…"

Ricardo inhaled a long raspy breath. Mike had heard that death rattle sound too often to forget it. He put his fingers to Ricardo's neck again and checked his pulse. As Ricardo exhaled, the interval between pulse beats lengthened and the throb of the artery weakened, like an echo dissipating in a canyon. A last feeble bump. Ricardo was gone.

Elena looked up at Mike. He shook his head. She collapsed into heaving sobs, Ricardo's hand to her cheek. Maria went to her side and began to cry. Mike flapped open one of the sheets and laid it over Ricardo's body. Red dots of blood blossomed on the snow-white surface.

Elena put Ricardo's hand in Maria's and stood up. She wiped the tears from her face. She took a deep breath, swallowed hard, and stared into Mike's eyes.

"You find Ramon for me," she said. "Bad men at Montedolores take one son from me, but not both."

"I'm sorry for Ricardo," Mike said, taken by surprise by the request. "*Lo siento mucho.* But I'm not the one you need. You need the police."

"*No policia*" she said, emphasizing her adamancy with a chopping hand motion. "*Son corruptos.* Only you I trust. You bring my Ramon home."

A memory flashed by of Ramon, the goofy kid with the big ears who worshipped his older brother.

"I can't do that Elena," Mike protested. "I'm just here to help the farmers. I don't have the authority you need."

Maria went to another table in the room. She picked up a pen and drew on the back of an old envelope. She returned and held it up in front of Mike.

"I see the pictures when I am cleaning," she said. "I see this sign. You can save my son. I trust you."

On the back of the envelope, she had drawn two crossed arrows, the insignia of the U.S. Special Forces. She must have seen some of the pictures he had from his Army days. Of course she would recognize the Special Forces. They had been all through this area years ago, to train the local army to fight a Marxist insurgency. They brought clean water and security to the valley. Those heroes could do anything.

But Mike knew he couldn't. He was old and tired. His body was stiff as starched khakis each morning. He depended on reading glasses. He hadn't run two miles in years, or fired a weapon in twice as long. The SF soldier she needed was someone a lot younger. He wanted to explain all this to her.

Hope and determination filled her face. Mike's flattered ego urged him to help. His compassion weighed in with the same recommendation. Common sense was outnumbered two-to-one.

"I'll go for him," he said to Elena. "I will bring back your Ramon."

The look on Elena's face melted from demanding to relieved. She hugged Mike, crying again, this time in gratitude.

"*Camina Dios con tu,*" she said. "Bring my boy home to me."

Mike hoped that he could.

◆◆◆

The Montedolores Plantation was legendary throughout Honduras, and even the world. The plantation scientists had genetically engineered a strain of spinach they called proteinich. It had spinach's high iron content, but the same level of protein as a plate of steak. They had also replaced the bitter spinach taste with a sweet flavor that most people found irresistible. This perfect high-protein, low-fat food swept into salads across the world. The plantation owners claimed it would only grow in the volcanic soil in their valley, and refused to allow anyone else to cultivate the plant. The cut leaves were irradiated to increase their shelf life. The process scrambled the plant's DNA. No outsider had been able to reproduce the little leaves. Montedolores held a complete monopoly, and the sprigs cost more per ounce than saffron. Yet demand among the world's elite grew, and rising output from the plantation never met demand.

The owners had carved their own kingdom in the jungle. The profits the plantation generated greased many greedy palms. Mike's first thought was that Ricardo had escaped from some horrific form of slave labor. If so, none of the corrupt government officials would intervene.

The plantation was sixty miles away from Mike's village, across two steep ridge lines. He planned on taking the USAID Ford most of the way there. He would hide it off plantation property and sneak in at night. Secrecy was the key. If the workers there were being treated like Ricardo, asking about it at the front office, even with U.S. government credentials, would be useless.

It was late afternoon when Mike's truck halted on the final ridge overlooking the plantation. The temperature had peaked, and Mike's brown T-shirt was soaked in sweat. His cut-off olive drab cargo shorts stuck to his legs. He unfolded a topographic map of the area.

He silently thanked God for satellites and the USGS. His work gave him access to the best maps of the area. The plantation sat on several hundred acres on the far side of the river below him. He pulled out a pair of binoculars.

A twelve-foot-high chain link fence surrounded the plantation. Razor wire spiraled through the top three feet. Vegetation for yards around the fence was stripped to the ground. A few armed, semi-uniformed guards patrolled the inner perimeter with unimpeded fields of fire. Mike had seen Iraqi prisons with less formidable barriers.

The steel mesh fence safeguarded row upon row of the small proteinich wonder plants within. A few low buildings dotted the farmland, but the rows were sown tight and straight to maximize yield. At one end, irrigation sprinklers doused a section of the crop, and left beautiful rainbows in their wake.

Mike always trained his soldiers on reconnaissance to note what they saw, but also what they *didn't* see. Other than the guards, he didn't see anyone within the plantation. No one tended the fields. No one drove tractors. No one harvested leaves. For a product shipped daily in guarded convoys, there wasn't much work being done to produce it.

Mike wondered what Ricardo and Ramon had been doing at the plantation. Maybe they had been guards instead of laborers. He scrutinized the guards through his binoculars. They wore random combinations of military uniforms and carried AK-47 assault rifles with disrespectful nonchalance. Mike categorized them immediately, the hulking death squad types supported by both the far right and left. Ramon and Ricardo could never run with those thugs. The two boys must have worked in the plantation. Mike bet Ramon was still there.

Going over the imposing perimeter fence would attract attention, especially his screams as the concertina wire at the top shredded his flesh. In the old days, he would have had tools to cut through the wire. Of course in the old days, he'd have had an entire A Team with him, air support on call and joints that didn't ache when he moved.

He spied an opportunity. An enormous discharge pipe ran under the fence, diverting irrigation runoff into the river. The river had scoured away the earth around the pipe at the fence line. With a little digging, he could get under the fence. The pipe would shield him from view while he dug. He'd be inside in minutes. Add in the cover of darkness, and the odds posted in his favor.

Mike pulled the truck deeper into the bush. From the back he grabbed a collapsible shovel and a webbed military belt. A long ammunition pouch filled with medical supplies hung from the belt's right side, a nine-inch sheathed hunting knife on the left. He pulled the K-Bar for inspection. Two gouges marred the otherwise razor-sharp edge.

"We're out of retirement for one last mission," he said.

In and out without firearms. Stealth would have to trump strength.

◆◆◆

By ten p.m., the setting moon left the valley in complete darkness. He'd timed the guards' rounds, and he had about twenty minutes between their perimeter patrols. He swam across the river. On the bank near the plantation, he tucked himself up against the side of the discharge pipe.

Mike reached down and grabbed a handful of the dark earth. He spread it across his face and neck to dull the natural shine of his skin. After years of painting his face with the hated Army camo sticks, here he was wishing for one. He smiled at the irony.

The guard passed again. His footsteps grew faint. Mike started to dig.

He noticed a rank, familiar smell. He stuck his head around and into the discharge pipe. He jerked it back. He expected the scent of fertilizer and chemicals from the plantation runoff. Instead, the pipe smelled like an outhouse. The plantation must also use the pipe for other waste. He congratulated himself on not planning to crawl through the tube. A central sanitation system seemed like a lot of expense for workers who grew up without toilets, but this was no time to ponder the plantation's infrastructure costs.

Footsteps shuffled along the inside of the fence line. Mike cursed and slinked into the shadows of the discharge pipe. The footsteps came closer. They stopped over Mike's head. The pungent aroma of hot spices excreted through sweaty pores wafted past him. The man's labored breathing wheezed through damaged lungs. Fresh sweat burst out on Mike's forehead.

Mike reached over and slipped his knife from its sheath. With one thrust, he could get one of the guard's vital organs through the fence, and then escape across the river. His heart beat faster. He held his breath and waited for the tell-tale snap of the safety release on the AK.

A lighter clicked twice. Harsh cigarette smoke drifted by, and the guard delivered a phlegm-clogged hack. Footsteps retreated. Mike exhaled. He slid the knife back in its sheath.

With a few minutes of digging, the hole was just wide enough to slide through. Leaving the shovel behind, he pulled himself up and into the empty plantation compound. A large steel shed, about twice the size of a tractor trailer rig, stood a few hundred yards ahead through the rows of proteinich. It had a man door on one side, a rollup door on the other and no windows. A large fuel tank sat on a steel frame outside the building. This was as good a place as any to start looking for Ramon. He crouched to reduce his silhouette, and ran for the building.

Halfway there, he leapt across two proteinich furrows. As he crested the second row, the plants scratched his bare legs. The leaves felt sharp and stiff, nothing like any relative of spinach he could imagine.

He stopped and went to one knee. He grabbed some of the leaves and pulled. The whole plant ripped out of the ground. It was fake. Eight plastic leaves glued into a buried black cube. The plants in the other row were the same. The whole field was sown with artificial plants.

A fake farm made no sense. The real proteinich came from somewhere. Guarded convoys of it left here daily.

The big rollup door on the shed in front of him opened. Mike dropped flat on the ground and watched through a frame of plastic leaves. An engine rumbled to life. Headlights pierced the darkness. A large cargo truck, one of the armored ones that hauled the precious proteinich, pulled out of the shed. The vehicle stopped, and the driver got out and closed the rollup door. He reentered the truck, and drove off to the main gate.

This was Mike's chance. The driver had to close the door himself, so the shed was unmanned. There were answers in there. He raced through the field and entered through the small side door.

A few stray bulbs dimly lit the shed. A gas pump stood against the rear wall. There was no loading dock, or any way to get large quantities of materials in or out of the shed. Mike briefly thought that it might be a maintenance area, but the dirt floor and the lack of tools shot that idea down. The usual trash cluttered the base of the walls; empty soda bottles, rags, a few rusty farming tools.

In the center of the shed, a metal tube protruded a foot from the ground. It was about five feet across with a hinged corrugated steel cover.

Mike walked over and raised the lid. A light burned twenty feet down at the bottom of the smooth, steel shaft. Ladder-type railings were welded to one side. A scent like a greenhouse rose out of the shaft, an earthy smell, like warm peat moss, tinged with something oddly antiseptic.

Maybe they were growing the stuff underground, like a fungus. He listened at the shaft and heard nothing. Whatever was going on down there did not appear to have a night shift. He climbed down.

The lower he got, the brighter the lighting became. At the base of the shaft was a small, white concrete hall. Two windowless push doors stood at the end of the hall, like the entrance to a hospital emergency room. The overpowering greenhouse smell turned Mike's stomach. He slid his knife from its sheath and moved to the end of the hall. He pushed open one of the doors.

He caught his breath. Beyond the doors was a low, wide cave. Both the ceiling and the walls looked hand-hewn out of solid rock. Harsh fluorescent lights lit the room. It stretched out for over a thousand yards.

Rows of stainless steel tables filled the cave. Naked people lay on their stomachs on each table. Men, women, and even children lay in rows, spread eagle. Each had an IV in one arm and a catheter running out and under the table. Most had their eyes open in vacant stares. Their near-transparent skin stretched over thin skeletal frames. Except for the gentle rising of their chests as they breathed, the room was eerily motionless. Mike winced at the sight of the victim's backs.

Leaves of proteinich sprouted from their shoulders to the base of their spines. The plant's roots, a mass of white filaments, were visible through the victims' pale skin.

Mike circled the tables in a state of shock. When the Montedolores spokesman told the newsmen the valley had special fertilizer for growing proteinich, he was not lying. On some people, the proteinich leaves had been harvested at least once. Neatly cut stems still protruded from their backs and a second growth of frilly heads popped up between them.

The horror of it all sank in. The complex proteins in the proteinich had to have a complex source. Some sick mind had genetically modified this abomination of a plant to thrive in protein, and then some sicker mind had figured out the cheapest source of protein most attuned to human assimilation. Death squads now had a market for the byproduct of terror. Instead of just being killed, captives were delivered alive by truck to the shed. Everyone made a profit.

Mike's throat tightened as he realized that Ricardo had been one of these table zombies just a few days ago. The courage of the boy tearing these carnivorous plants from his own back...

Then he thought of Ramon. He scanned the tables for that familiar face. Three rows over, he recognized Ramon's big jug ears.

He hurried to his side, already calculating if he could get the boy's weight up the access shaft to the shed. As he got closer, his jaw sagged open. Ramon looked hideous. His skin had developed a greenish tint. Roots filled his body cavity and stretched the skin away from his ribs in thick green lumps. Pale root tips protruded from his ears and nose.

Bile burned in Mike's throat. Ramon was too far gone. He'd promised Elena he'd save him.

He could at least save him from this living hell. It would be a favor to Ramon to end his life. He looked at the hundreds of living corpses around him. It would be a favor to them all. He gave Ramon's hair a light pass with his fingertips.

"You will see Ricardo soon," he said.

Mike sheathed his knife and ran back through the doors to the hallway. He burst through and stopped dead.

A young, unkempt guard in a camouflage muscle shirt stood a foot away with an incredulous look on his face. He pointed his AK at Mike from the waist.

"*¿Quien es?*"

Mike spun around, grabbed the gun barrel and tucked the AK under his armpit. He charged backwards and slammed the guard into the wall. His skull cracked against concrete and he groaned.

A spray of rounds burst from the AK. The bullets shattered the doors to the cave. The barrel went hot in Mike's hands, but he clamped down and yanked the weapon free from the guard. Without looking, he slammed the butt stock back twice into the guard's face. Blood gushed from his nose, and the guard slid to the floor, unconscious.

Mike dropped the rifle. Burns traced the creases of his palms. He cursed his slow reaction time and sloppy exit from the cave. Someone probably heard that gunfire. His escape clock just started ticking.

He scrambled up the access shaft to the shed. Every grip of a rung sent new flashes of pain from his palms. Back in the garage, he picked up a bottle from the pile of debris and filled it with gasoline from the pump. He set the bottle down and snaked the fuel hose through the dirt to the access shaft. He pulled a bandage from the ammo pouch on his belt and tied the fuel nozzle trigger open. Gasoline gushed from the nozzle and filled the air with its sweet, metallic scent. He dropped the nozzle down the access shaft.

Spattering fuel echoed from the shaft's concrete floor. Gasoline ran down the short hallway and under the door to the cave. A pool formed under the tables of torture. Volatile fumes crowded the cave, begging for a reason to explode. When they did, the blast would suck all the oxygen from the room. Every living thing, plant and animal, would die.

Mike stuffed another bandage into the gasoline-filled bottle's neck. He pulled a lighter from his ammo pouch. He flicked it on and touched the flame to the rag. Fire raced through the cloth.

"Forgive me, Ramon," he said.

He cocked his arm and threw the bottle. It arced liked a shooting star across the shed and disappeared down the access tube.

Mike hit the ground and covered his ears. A huge blast rumbled underneath him. A fireball erupted from the access tube, and mushroomed up against the shed's ceiling. Searing heat singed the back of his neck. The sickly-sweet smell of burning flesh filled the air.

Mike burst through the shed door and sprinted into the night. He ran straight for the drainpipe at the fence. If he didn't escape in the first few moments of confusion, he never would.

Excited shouting in Spanish rose from all around the plantation. Flames engulfed the shed. Other distant buildings on the plantation burst like torches in the darkness, set afire by access to the subterranean inferno.

Two guards ran in Mike's direction. He hit the ground and rolled under the meager protection of a row of plastic plants. The guards rushed by him, fixated on the burning building. Minutes later he crossed the river and headed home.

♦♦♦

Mike waited until morning to see Elena. She took the news stoically, as Mike told her that he was too late to save Ramon. Perhaps she had resigned herself to the death of her younger son. Perhaps she just had no more grief left to give. For now.

"*Gracias, Seňor C.*," she said. "You try to help Ramon. I am grateful."

Ω

Premonitions

"Alfie, what is all this?"

Stan poked through a pile of photographs and handwritten notes on Alfie's cheap kitchen table. The battered manila envelope next to them was still half full.

"That's what I needed to talk to you about," Alfie said.

Alfie rubbed his tense, sweating palms against his thighs. His chair creaked as his right leg shuddered in time with his racing pulse. Tension filled every corner of Alfie's claustrophobic apartment to the bursting point. It was a big gamble, letting Stan in on this. If his brother would support him, just this once ...

Stan picked up a picture from the top of the pile. The tips of his thin fingers held it by the corner, as if some infectious disease might pervade the photo. A few locks of his perfectly coiffed hair dipped down into his field of view and he swept them back with his free hand. He studied the picture with first alarm and then sadness.

The picture had the grainy texture of a cell phone snapshot blown up to three times normal size. The woman in it was dirty blonde, in her late twenties, with blue eyes and a petite nose that came to a slight upturned point. Her long, wild hair was temporarily tamed into a ponytail by a bright red scarf. She walked through Central Park in the surreptitiously shot candid picture.

"So who is she?" Stan said.

Alfie shifted in his seat. He hitched his pants up a bit. They were now at least a size too large. He gave the dark stubble on his chin a nervous scratch.

"Well, it's going to be hard to explain, so you need to listen first..."

Stan looked down at the pile of pictures. One by one, he flicked them across the table with his index finger, each photo a bit faster than the last. They were all of the same woman. Entering a subway station. Walking along Madison Avenue. Sipping coffee with another woman at an outdoor café.

"Jesus, Alfie, are you some kind of stalker?"

"No, no. I'm not stalking her. She's stalking me. In my dreams."

Stan dropped the picture like it was white hot. He stepped back from the table, back from Alfie. His lips tightened into that disapproving grimace Alfie had seen on his older brother's face so many times before. Alfie pushed himself up out of his chair, as if he had to head off his brother's escape.

"Now, Stan. Hear me out. For once, don't shut me down."

"Alfie, this is way around the bend."

"No, look. It started a few months ago. I started having dreams. Dreams so real you could touch them. Perfect clarity, down to smells. Beautiful dreams in wonderful places around the city. The Aquarium, botanical gardens, museums, along the Hudson. In every dream, she was there." He pointed at the pictures on the table. "Over and over. Every time."

"Dreams are just dreams."

"But then it got worse. They turned from dreams to visions. I'd get flashes during the day. Snippets that would just jump into my head. I'd see her sleeping, the morning sun on her face. Or a few seconds of her cooking something at the stove here in my apartment. And every time, I'd get this warm feeling of love, of completeness."

Stan started to look frightened. Alfie rushed to explain.

"So I figured that this must be a sign, a premonition of good things to come, of an end to being alone. Several of these flashes took place in and around the Museum of Natural History and Central Park. So I guessed she must be there a lot. So I started spending the afternoons there after work."

"You spent every afternoon wandering around the outside of the museum? You're lucky you weren't arrested for planning a robbery or something."

"Then one afternoon, I saw her leaving the museum. She carried books and a messenger bag, like she worked there."

Alfie replayed the moment in his mind. The rush of adrenaline, the pounding of his heart, the unwarranted surge of complete familiarity and fulfillment. Just thinking of it made his skin tingle. He sorted through a few pages of his handwritten notes.

"From there, it didn't take much to learn who she was. Linda Latsko. Assistant Curator of Minerals."

Herself a diamond, he added to himself.

85

Stan rushed the table and grabbed the handwritten page and gave it a panicked once over.

"You have her address, her phone number, her email? Are you insane? This is wrong about ten different ways, and as a lawyer, I can tell you it's a borderline felony."

"You don't understand," Alfie said. "You haven't seen her in the visions. The way she smiles at me, the way she feels when I hold her hand, the look in her eyes when I tell her I love her. This is like nothing I've ever experienced before."

"Neither is a year in Riker's, which is what this will earn you," Stan said. "She's a total stranger."

"Who's also always alone. She lives alone, just goes to work and back every day, waiting for the right one."

"Damn it, Alfie, are you camping outside her window? You dreamed up some fantasy blonde, then came across someone who looked similar. Wow, in crowded New York City, big surprise. Then you hammered all these pieces together, and built up this whole thing in your mind."

"What if I didn't?" Alfie said. "What if I'm seeing premonitions of our future together? What if she's seeing the same thing?"

"Jesus!" Stan threw his hands up in the air. The handwritten page sailed off toward the kitchen. "You won't end up in Riker's, you'll end up in Bellevue. Are you listening to yourself?"

"I know it will work out," Alfie said. He stood and pulled a narrow envelope from his back pocket. His voice turned dreamy. "The rest is all arranged. The getaway we've both been dreaming of."

Stan snatched the envelope from his hands. Inside were two plane tickets to Hawaii. One carried the name of Linda Latsko.

"You're out of your damn mind!" Stan said. "You make minimum wage. How did you pay for these?"

"I've been saving." Alfie's voice drifted back into reverie. "There's something that binds us all together. Currents that can push us in the right direction, if we are smart enough to not swim against them. That's what's happening here. I'm getting a message, a preview of our future together. And I know she is too. Once we finally meet—"

Stan grabbed him by the shoulders. His face turned red and he shook his little brother.

"Don't even think about it! You hear me! You'll scare this poor woman to death with this crazy story. She'll call a cop, or mace you, or maybe even shoot you, if she's armed. She's not your soul mate. She's a stranger. She's not dreaming of you!"

Alfie's head hurt from the shaking. His brother's fingers dug hot divots in his upper arms.

"Okay! Okay! I get it. You're hurting me!"

Stan let him go and took a deep breath. "I'm sorry. Everything you're saying just scares the hell out of me. This fuse your imagination has lit goes straight to a keg of dynamite. I've seen this kind of thing in court all the time. Don't I always look out for you?"

"Well, yes."

"Then promise me you won't approach this woman again."

Alfie sighed. "Okay. I won't. I promise."

Stan stuffed the notes, tickets and pictures into the manila envelope and shoved it under his arm. "And I'll take care of this mess, which is good for a misdemeanor, minimum."

Stan left in a hurry.

Alfie feared from the beginning Stan wouldn't be convinced. He had to try anyway. He'd hoped that maybe this one time, his big brother would take a leap of faith about something, instead of having to have that "preponderance of evidence" he always talked about. Too much to hope for. His brother was a hard facts kind of guy.

Alfie would just have to talk with Linda tomorrow, and get those hard facts.

◆◆◆

Alfie spied Linda at a corner table on the Verdant Café's patio, where she met her friend Connie for lunch every Friday. She always arrived at a quarter to twelve, Connie at noon. Linda wore a dark brown patterned dress that ended just past her knees. The familiar dress was one of his favorites. A good omen.

His window of opportunity opened. A public place, in daylight, where she'd feel safe. She'd recognize him from her dreams, but be unsure how to admit it, until he told her that she haunted his as well. Then they could both relax and relish the moment, the moment when they both began the rest of their lives.

Alfie tucked a few stray hairs back behind his ear. He straightened his tie, an uncomfortable addition for his crucial first real-life impression. He took a deep breath and marched past the gate into the outdoor dining area.

Linda's face was buried in her slab-sided menu. Alfie stopped next to her table. His mouth went dry. Nervous muscles in his arms twitched.

"Linda?" he nearly whispered.

Linda looked up. Her mouth dropped open. The menu hit the table with a thud that rattled the silverware. Alfie raised his hands in surrender.

"Sorry, didn't mean to startle you."

The moment was here. Her stunned reaction could mean only one thing. His knees locked in anticipation of her jubilant response to his next question.

"Do you recognize me?"

Her eyes went wide, though it did not seem with joy. Then they darted about the café, as if searching for an exit. She straightened up in her seat and looked back to the menu on the table.

"No, I don't. You must have me confused with someone else."

He'd half-expected that answer. He might have said the same if their roles were reversed. He sat in the chair Connie always took.

"It's okay. I know you know who I am. I've been trying to find you for so long."

Heavy hands clamped down on his shoulders and pressed him into his seat. Linda jumped up and back so quickly that her chair skidded practically into the street. She looked to Alfie's left with fire in her eyes.

"What the hell is this?" she yelled as she pointed at Alfie.

Alfie looked up. Two uniformed police officers held him in place. His brother stood to the left. The three were panting.

"I'm so sorry," Stan said to Linda. "We lost him on the subway. He shouldn't have gotten this far. This really wasn't supposed to happen."

"You're damn right it isn't supposed to happen. I'd have never agreed to the plea bargain if crap like this was going to happen. You promised that the memory wipe would be permanent."

"It is, sort of. He only thinks he knows who you are."

Alfie's head started to spin. None of this made any sense.

"You said I wouldn't have to leave the city," Linda said. "I'd be anonymous in nine million people. Does this look anonymous to you?"

"Stan?" Alfie said. "You know her?"

"He's not dangerous," Stan said to Linda.

"Liar! The obsessive son of a bitch tried to kill me with a meat cleaver! You think I don't remember that?"

Alfie shook his head as he tried to rise. "No, Linda, I would never—"

The cops shoved him down harder.

"I'll take him back to the Institute," Stan said. "They'll give him another treatment. Stronger, this time."

"Forget it! I've already spent too many years of my life with him. I'm not spending the rest of it worrying he'll return. It's bad enough that my trust issues keep me alone as it is. I rescind my consent, as the judge's sentence allowed. Send him back to prison."

She swept her purse off the ground and stomped off down the sidewalk. The two cops hoisted Alfie to his feet. Every patron in the café stared at Alfie in silent shock. Alfie watched the woman of his dreams disappear into the crowd. His knees went weak.

"Stan," Alfie pleaded, "I don't understand what's going on."

"And the sad thing is," Stan said with a shake of his head, "you probably never will. Unless the bad memories eventually surface with the good. Memory wipes are experimental treatment for obsessive behavior. I got you off of an attempted murder charge with an insanity plea, as long as you agreed to the treatment. It's supposed to erase the obsession, and eliminate you being a danger to society."

"I tried to kill Linda?" Alfie couldn't believe it.

"When she left you for someone else," Stan said. "This violates the condition of your parole. Now the situation's out of my hands. You couldn't listen to me and leave her alone. Don't I always look out for you?"

◆◆◆

I read a story in the news about scientists who manipulated the memories of mice. I seemed to be the only person concerned with the implications, like no one else ever saw the movie Total Recall.

We can only be better people by learning from the mistakes and sad memories from our pasts. Too bad.

Ω

Kindred Spirits

"You'd better not start doing this."

"Doing what?"

"Canceling out on me and hiding out in the bush."

Karin pulled her Land Rover over to the side of the road. This conversation with her best friend Trisha would take more concentration than she could spare on the rutted roads across the South African savannah.

"Trish, for the last time, I'm not hiding," she said into her cell phone. "My clinic is out here. I live here."

"But you need to come down to Durbin," Trisha said. "See some bright lights and let off some steam."

"Look, something came up today that I need to take care of, that's all."

"If it has anything to do with crawling back to your soon-to-be-ex," Trisha said, "I'll drive up there and stomp you."

"Damn, Trish, you should know better than that." Karin's last six months had been hell. Her rat bastard husband Brent had left her for a twenty-something with frazzled platinum hair and brains to match. The bitch was named Candice, but preferred "Candy". Please. "The terms were set yesterday at the mediation."

"And you didn't tell me?" Trisha said. She gave Karin a punishing blast from the "#" key on her phone. "All the more reason we need to celebrate tonight! What did you get out of the deal?"

"Everything."

"What do you mean, 'everything'?"

"Three quarters of the assets, the clinic, the house and the vehicles here. He keeps the Land Cruiser and the condo in Johannesburg. Judy stays with me when she returns from Manchester this summer." Their daughter Judy had opted for a year abroad with relatives in England for her eighth grade year. "He was so busy letting his dick do his thinking that he'd have signed anything."

"We *have* to celebrate," Trisha pleaded. "Tonight."

"Later," Karin said. "I promise. Gotta go."

She hung up before Trisha could reply. She didn't want to have to explain why she took the long cross-province trip to the Stevenson reserve.

The lopsided divorce settlement was quite fair in Karin's eyes. After all, though Brent's money had started her veterinary clinic, she had built the practice up from scratch, while he'd spent most weeks trading stocks in the city. She felt no guilt in keeping the business she created. So she was a little ahead in the financial assets. Well, screw the philandering loser on that one.

She checked herself in the rearview mirror. Her tawny hair was in a loose ponytail and the bright sunlight lit her blue eyes a shade of aquamarine. A strict regimen of protecting her fair skin from the African sun meant she looked a decade younger than her true age of forty-two. Still not as young as the Bimbo Bitch, but brains had to count for something at some point.

An hour later she arrived at Stevenson's private reserve. He bred black rhinos for a living and tended "retired" elephants with the profits. All the pachyderms were female and most were rescued from circuses and zoos that had gone under. A few had been orphaned or turned in by idiots who bought calves for pets.

Ranji, a short Indian man in his twenties, met Karin outside the main building. Ranji had risen to become Stevenson's right hand man.

"Dr. Karin," Ranji said, concern in his voice. "I did not know we needed your services."

"You don't," Karin said. "I was just in the neighborhood, and thought I'd visit the girls."

"Ah, a social visit." Ranji smiled. "You needn't have traveled so far."

Karin laughed at Ranji's running joke. Elephants communicated across great distances through sub-sonic rumblings, probably received through their feet. Ranji believed people could tune in to them if they tried.

A high, reinforced fence, like a prop from *Jurassic Park*, enclosed acres of scrub. A half dozen elephants surrounded a pond several hundred yards away. Two small calves stood in the water up to their necks. One sprayed the other from its trunk, and a mini-rainbow flickered in the mist. The adults alternated between keeping a watchful eye on the horizon and plucking strands of acacia browse from artificial steel trees.

"The calves were orphaned in Kruger Park," Ranji said. "But the ladies took to them right away."

Off to the left, one elephant stood alone in a separate, smaller enclosure. A bale of hay sat on the ground untouched. Even with the herd far away, it was clear she was larger than the rest. She was the reason for Karin's trip.

She was Tillie, graciously shortened from Waltzing Matilda the Dancing Elephant. The former star of Amazo's Carnival had mastered the elephantine versions of the flamenco and the waltz, a study in grace despite bulk. The carnival folded after the owner's trailer rolled down a hill one night and killed him. Stevenson had taken the abandoned pachyderm into his herd. She ascended to become the herd's matriarch, a stern mother who kept the members protected and in line.

"Tillie is alone?" Karin said. She had a soft spot for the animal. At the carnival, Tillie had held vehicles aloft while mechanics worked on them, and other times even handed them tools. Elephants that well-trained were a pleasure to work with.

"Yes," Ranji said. "She had to be separated after what happened to Zara."

"I heard a bit about that," Karin said to prime the information pump.

"We took Zara in last month," Ranji said, "a hand-raised rescue. She was but a teenager, yet she pushed Tillie for dominance."

"Tillie won't be pushed," Karin said.

"No indeed," Ranji said. "And Zara was smaller. One would think that she would find her place. But she would not join the herd, unless she led it.

"When Tillie caught her trying to direct the herd to a different watering station, there was a fight. Zara would not back down, even after she was injured. Tillie crushed her, pounded her flat like she used to dance the flamenco."

Karin always sensed Tillie had great inner strength and a commitment to the herd. But malice? It didn't seem in an elephant's nature.

"Mr. Stevenson does not trust her," Ranji said. "He will not let her back with the herd."

Karin approached Tillie's enclosure.

"You must not get too close," Ranji warned.

Karin felt no danger. Tillie turned to her, and stepped to the fence. Ranji backed away. Karin stared into Tillie's big brown eye, framed by long black lashes. Karin felt her feet hum. She saw her reflection in the elephant's pupil, as if she was also on the other side.

Karin understood what had happened, she more than anyone. The younger elephant threatened Tillie's family. Tillie hadn't struck out in anger, but in defense.

The low hum worked up past Karin's knees. She reached a hand through the steel bars. Tillie tossed a pinch of dust in the air with her trunk. Then she bent her head for Karin to touch.

Up close, the fine hairs that declared Tillie a mammal glistened in the sun. Karin ran her fingers across the bridge of Tillie's trunk. Her skin felt tough, but Karin knew the truth, that it was as sensitive as her own, prone to sunburn and infection. An elephant wasn't as indestructible as it looked.

I understand you, she thought.

Tillie plucked a blade of grass from the ground. She snaked her trunk up and around Karin's arm with a surprisingly gentle caress. She dropped the blade of grass into Karin's palm. Tillie exhaled and her warm breath ruffled the hairs on the vet's arm. The hum at Karin's knees rose into her chest.

Karin turned to Ranji. "I'll take her with me," she said.

"I'm sorry?"

"I know how cautious George is. He'll worry about Tillie's risk to the herd, his ability to continue to accept rescues. If he's going to keep her from her herd, it's torture to keep her within sight of it. She'll come to my ranch with me."

"I doubt severely that Mr. Stevenson…" Ranji began.

She withdrew her arm from the fence and patted Ranji's arm. "I'll take care of George."

♦♦♦

George Stevenson was easier to convince than Karin had thought. He loaned her a trailer and she drove Tillie home that day.

Her clinic was already set up for elephants, as she had treated several.

Tillie bolted from the trailer as soon as the gate dropped. She announced her arrival with a mighty trumpet, lest any animals within earshot doubt that a new dominant species was in town.

Tillie's enclosure was between the main house and the clinic, easy to view from Karin's second floor bedroom. Karin checked on her several times that first night. Each time, Tillie was staring up at Karin's window.

Within weeks, they had their routine. Each morning at eight AM, Karin would throw the twin bolts on the gate and let Tillie roam free. The elephant would stay near the house, her food and her watering trough. Only when Karin would go for a ramble in the savannah would Tillie leave the yard, and then just to follow her owner.

Even with Brent gone and Judy in England, the compound had been far from lonely. She had assistants who started work at nine AM, and clients came and went all day to check on the animals left in her care. But Tillie's presence made Karin realize something had been missing.

Brent, prior to his mid-life-crisis-total-jackass transformation, had made the house a home. He and Karin had shared a bond that imbued the house with a life force commercial structures never knew. Judy's birth had enhanced that feeling. It was as if her growing up there gave the home deeper roots. The twin strikes of Judy's absence and the collapse of Karin's marriage had stripped the building of that magic essence.

Tillie's arrival breathed that life back into the structure. The elephant was ever available when Karin needed a spot of company. Throughout the day, Tillie's occasional rumble or snort from the outside reassured Karin that she was not alone.

Karin never followed up on that city date with Trisha.

◆◆◆

Sundays were "emergency only" days at the clinic, and Karin spent these days unwinding from the stress of the week. One Sunday she opted for a post-dawn hike culminating in breakfast at a rocky outcropping south of her clinic. She packed herself a light meal and a few of Tillie's favorite fruits.

On the way to the door, she passed the flashing answering machine. Sixth message that week. All from Brent. He wanted to talk. She wanted him to go to hell. This was too nice a day to deal with him. She pressed "delete" and walked out the door.

When she threw the bolts and swung wide the gate to Tillie's enclosure, the elephant uncharacteristically stepped back.

"Tillie, come on."

Tillie responded with a rumble. She gave the ground two sharp swats with her trunk.

"No walking this morning, Tillie?"

Tillie brought one big brown eye to bear on Karin.

"OK, girl. I'm going out. Stay back if you want." She slung her pack over her shoulder and headed off to the bush. Tillie could roam around the house grounds.

The crisp clear morning fit Karin's mood with perfection. The months since the divorce had helped assuage the betrayal and heartbreak. Judy had volunteered to return home but Karin wouldn't hear of it. Knowing her daughter offered was support enough. Business was good and Tillie had given her life a new dimension, as if the addition of an elephant's perspective had changed hers.

Rains earlier in the week had triggered an explosion of wildflowers and given the other bushes a far deeper green than usual. The air smelled alive, and butterflies danced from flower to flower. Karin realized that she hadn't allowed herself to be lost in the beauty of Africa lately, too focused on the dark shadows of divorce. She closed her eyes and drank in a deep breath of the spring's sweet scents.

The trumpet of an elephant shattered the silence. Karin snapped out of her reverie in time to see Tillie thunder past her. Karin's hair ruffled in Tillie's wake.

A muffled roar exploded from the tall grass between two lala palms. A lioness rose from her hunter's crouch. The cat's head swiveled to face Tillie's charge, canines wet and white. Her claws dug into the earth.

But the big cat knew she met her match. She bounded away with an irritated snarl. Tillie jerked to a stop where the lioness had lain in wait. She stomped her feet rapid fire in a final dominant display.

Karin rushed to Tillie's side and hugged the elephant's leg. "Tillie. Thank God," she sighed.

Tillie swung her trunk across Karin's shoulder. Karin had seen elephants charge prides of lions to defend the family. Now Karin was family. Tillie had no doubt smelled the lioness while Karin's less sensitive nose had grown drunk on pollen. Karin had committed the cardinal sin of unforgiving Africa. She'd taken her safety for granted. This wasn't lioness territory, but the rains would have replenished watering holes, and spurred a shift in the wildlife patterns. She should have realized that. If it hadn't been for Tillie…

Tillie turned and cast a reproachful eye over Karin. Karin bowed her head in embarrassment. The elephant flapped her great ears, raised her trunk into an 'S", and headed back for the house. She swatted Karin with her tail, the way elephants herd calves. Karin followed. She stroked Tillie's tail as it swished past.

◆◆◆

The next morning, a knock at the door startled Karin. None of her staff was due for an hour. She opened the door to the last person in the world she wanted to see.

"Brent," she said. She could not disguise the cool revulsion in her voice for her ex-husband.

He looked thinner. He wore one of his white button down shirts, a far cry from the wild T-shirts he'd adopted when he'd first taken up with Candice. The dopey grin he'd had during the start of his courtship was gone.

"Karin. We've got something to discuss."

"I've got a phone. You know the number. I know how to let you roll to voicemail."

"I noticed as much. We need to talk this in person."

Karin peered past his shoulder. His Land Cruiser was parked in the driveway. Candy stood next to it in a pair of red shorts about six inches too high for savannah common sense. Her hair now sported a green stripe and a tight set of curls. With a look of terrified disgust, she waved both hands to shoo an insect from her face.

Karin balled her fists at the sight of her and set her jaw.

"She's staying out there," Brent reassured. "Can we talk inside for a moment?"

Karin would have rather stepped out and found out what The Bitch thought gave her the right to set foot on her property. But that would certainly lead to violence. She took a deep breath and stepped back. Brent walked in and closed the door.

"Look, I've been talking to my attorney," he started. Karin's heart sank. "He can't believe what I agreed to in our mediation."

"But you did."

Karin walked to the rear of the house. Brent followed.

"Well, he's certain that if we got to court, given the woeful undervaluation of the clinic business, I can get the mediation set aside and nearly all the assets back." He gave the interior of the house a once over. "Maybe even the house."

"The hell you will," Karin spat. "I'll spend every dime I've got to keep you from getting any of it."

"Easy," Brent said, his hands raised in defense. "I came here so we could talk through a more equitable solution, without getting lawyers involved. Especially around Judy's custody."

"Custody!" Karin practically caught fire.

"Candy thinks with some time together, Judy could understand the whole situation better."

Now Karin *was* ready to beat that woman senseless. Trying to tear what's left of her family apart? There's no way…

A scream rose from the front of the house. Brent's eyes went wide. He ran to the front door and yanked it open.

Candice lay a dozen yards from the Land Cruiser. A puddle of blood spread under her chest. Brent screamed and ran to her side. He lifted her head but her glassy, vacant eyes said she was dead.

◆◆◆

The police and the game warden both responded to Karin's emergency call. They questioned Karin and Brent separately, and got the same story. Karin's first thought had been about the lioness she'd encountered the day before, but it had been no cat attack. Candice had been crushed. Whatever had done it had some serious mass. The ground held the vaguest of prints. Tillie was safely caged, so the ranger guessed a rhino. The rains had set the whole province on a miniature migration and he'd seen a greater variety of wildlife over the last few days than he'd seen in a month. A city girl would have no idea how to deal with a rhino. If she had spooked it, it would have charged.

Karin closed the clinic that day. When the investigation wrapped and everyone left, Karin sat on the porch and tried to make sense of the morning's twists. She doubted that Brent would be back to talk about money again. He certainly would not want to live in the house where his girlfriend was killed.

It was near noon when she realized she'd never let Tillie out of her enclosure. Tillie waited next to the gate.

"Tillie, I'm so sorry. It's been crazy. Do you want to come out?"

Tillie responded with a low rumble.

Karin threw the top bolt of the gate. She reached down for the second bolt.

It was already thrown. She was certain she'd locked it the night before.

Karin pulled open the gate. Tillie bowed her head. The big brown eyes looked into Karin's. Deep in those dark recesses, Karin again felt that bond they shared, but this time uncomfortably so. The black lashes made a long slow sweep. Karin looked down.

Drops of blood speckled Tillie's nails.

"Oh God. No."

Tillie rested her trunk across Karin's shoulders. The hairs on Karin's neck went to attention. Tillie brought one eye inches from Karin's. Tillie's lashes flickered against Karin's brow. That low frequency hum vibrated Karin's whole body. She twitched in fear.

What the hell should I do now? she thought. Call the rangers? The police? Who would believe that I didn't put Tillie up to the murder?

They would even think that was the reason she'd picked Tillie up from Stevenson in the first place. She'd get arrested. And what would they do with Tillie? They'd shoot her on the spot.

Tillie wrapped her trunk around Karin's neck.

A thought popped into Karin's head. Didn't the home wrecking bitch deserve it? Didn't Brent rate a little suffering? No one suspects anything, and the investigation is as good as closed.

The rumble in Karin's chest rose to a low roar.

"No one will know," she whispered in Tillie's massive ear. "You were protecting me. Like from the lioness."

Tillie's trunk relaxed its grip.

Karin headed into the clinic for a bucket of soapy water and a stiff brush.

◆◆◆

The next week passed quietly. Clients were few, as they either avoided the scene of the murder or the discomfort of discussing it with Karin. She dismissed the staff for lack of work by two PM each day. Thoughts of the low traffic's impact on her business should have worried her. It did not.

Karin spent each afternoon with Tillie. The secret they shared now tethered them together. Karin could not sort through the mix of guilt and exultation that she experienced when she thought about Candy's death. But standing next to Tillie, feeling that soft hum in her stomach that the elephant broadcast, the confusion dissipated and the world seemed to right itself.

The lioness incident must have permanently spooked the elephant, for she would not walk the trails. Nor would she let Karin. When three tons of elephant block the way, there is no departure. Instead they lounged in the yard, Tillie in the shadow of the house, Karin in the shade of a pachyderm eclipse. Karin would read. Tillie would watch the horizon and emit the occasional low rumble that Karin knew meant all was well.

Dusk fell on Friday, and Karin came out of the house after dinner to lead Tillie back to her enclosure. She gave Tillie a pat on the trunk. Tillie ruffled her ears. Karin turned and the elephant followed her into the pen.

Karin gave the area a quick once over for water and an acacia snack. Behind her the gate slammed closed. She turned to see Tillie's trunk slither back from the gate.

"Tillie! What are you doing?"

Tillie raised her chin and flapped her ears with a snap, a classic elephant show of defiance. Karin headed to the gate. Tillie stepped in her way.

"Tillie, I need to go in and sleep."

Tillie snorted. Her trunk reached out to Karin's waist and pushed. The shove wasn't violent, but it was firm, surprisingly so from an appendage that could pluck a single leaf from a tree. It was the push a mother gave a youngster to get them where they needed to go, with just enough force to say she meant business. Karin took a few steps back and felt something brush against her feet.

She stood in straw. Not a pile, but a well-placed oval of uniform depth. A nest.

"Tillie, I can't sleep here. I have a house. You have —"

Tillie rolled her head around so that one eye lined up with Karin's. The intensity of the stare made Karin waver. Tillie's trunk touched Karin's shoulder and pressed down. A shiver of fear ran through Karin.

"OK, girl," she said. She dropped to one knee. The trunk kept pushing. "Just one night." She sat down on the straw. The rough stalks scraped her skin.

Tillie raised her trunk into an "S" and sniffed the air. Satisfied, she took a step back against the gate and stared at Karin. Karin reclined into a fetal position and closed her eyes.

She doubted she would sleep. Through her closed eyes she still felt the elephant's burning gaze. Her stomach hummed.

◆◆◆

It was March before Trisha finally came to visit, and she had to extend her own invitation. She saw why when she arrived. The place looked like hell. Weeds poked through every landscaped bed, and most of the bushes had withered to brown husks. The clinic was uncharacteristically quiet, missing the usual overnight patients.

Her friend didn't look much better. Karin's recessed eyes had a blank look. Her cheeks were sunken. Her frazzled hair hadn't seen conditioner in forever. Her clothes were so wrinkled she may have slept in them.

Tillie stood at the edge of the yard and smoothed the ground with her foot. She stared at the horizon.

"It's so peaceful out here," Trisha said, trying to find a compliment for the place. She sat on Karin's porch in sleek designer jeans and a tight blue polo shirt. She topped off her lemonade from the pitcher on the table between them.

"That's why I like it," Karin said. "See why I keep putting off a trip to the city?"

The word was that Karin put off smaller trips as well. Her staff went on supply runs without her, even for personal necessities and food.

"So when is daughter Judy coming back?"

"In a week," Karin said. "But we thought it was best that she stay with Brent."

Trisha nearly spit her lemonade onto the porch. "You must be kidding!"

"No," Karin said with an unconvincing shake of her head. "She's starting high school and bigger classes will be better."

Karin shot a nervous glance across at the elephant. Tillie turned her head just enough for her ear to face the house.

"It's not weird having an elephant around all the time?" Trisha asked.

"She's family," Karin said with a forced smile.

Something was horribly wrong here. Trisha had to get Karin into a different environment. The bush was getting to her.

"Well," Trisha said, "nice as this is here, you do still owe me a visit. Ride back with me. I'll get us theater tickets and I've got an eligible bachelor at work who is just your type."

Tillie shuffled closer to the porch. Karin gripped the arm of her chair.

"No, no," Karin said. "I've got patients scheduled tomorrow morning. Another time."

Trisha made a few more futile tries to convince Karin to leave her house. The sun dipped to the horizon, and she had to start the long trip back. As she drove away, she watched the odd, retreating scene in the rearview mirror. Her old friend on the porch, obviously depressed in the aftermath of her divorce, and an elephant, now next to the house. If Trisha didn't know better, she'd think Dumbo was on guard.

Under Trisha's car, a dirty, torn brake line dripped black fluid onto the gravel road.

Back at the house, Tillie wrapped her trunk around the porch railing and rubbed clean the faint greasy stripe along the tip.

Ω

Wages of Sin

Holy Thursday was the wrong day for this confrontation. It was almost 4:00 pm. Frank Murphy only had an hour before meeting his family for the Vigil Mass tonight. But he didn't have a choice. For weeks, he'd worried about the accounting irregularities he'd found. He couldn't take it anymore. Mr. DiAngelo had to be told.

Frank sat in a hard plastic chair outside the door to his boss's office, an unmarked manila folder in his lap. Sunrise Charities didn't splurge on furniture, or office amenities, or staff for that matter. The office was tucked into a rundown strip mall on Miami's Tamiani Trail. That frugality was one reason Frank had sought the job here, even though it was a pay cut from his position at Wachovia. Sunrise Charities' money went to help the homeless, feed the hungry, cure the sick. Frank wanted to be part of that, to use his CPA to make a difference in something other than a shareholder's report. All the more reason the potential fraud he'd uncovered had to be exposed.

Frank massaged the Knights of Columbus ring on his right hand, a nervous habit he'd been trying to break. The hour hand hit twelve on the big wall clock. 4:00. Showtime.

Frank stood and straightened his tie. The rest of the office was empty, getting an early start to the Easter holiday. Just as well. The fewer people that overheard the allegations, the better. He hoped Mr. DiAngelo would explain them all. He knocked on the boss's door and entered.

Mr. DiAngelo sat at his desk, a well-worn wooden model that looked like a cast off classroom teacher's desk. Haphazard piles of papers and books lay on dented filing cabinets. The sole narrow window had a fine view of an adjacent brick wall. A high backed chair faced the desk's front. White fuzz blossomed from the split across the leather seat.

Mr. DiAngelo's clothing was as unpretentious as his surroundings. Unless the boss was pitching a donor, he never wore a suit. Today, he wore a long sleeve denim shirt over a pair of far more faded jeans. As usual, his shirt's top button was buttoned, a quirk Frank always thought had to be uncomfortable. Mr.

DiAngelo's trademark thick black sandals stuck out near the front of the desk. He looked about thirty, with olive skin. His black hair was parted on the right with razor sharpness and slicked back. He looked up at Frank with a smile.

"Right on time," Mr. DiAngelo said. "A punctual accountant. It should go without saying. Have a seat."

Frank nodded and took the seat in front of the desk. He placed the manila envelope in his lap. "Thanks for making time for me, Mr. DiAngelo."

"I usually work late on this day each year," Mr. DiAngelo said. "But even if I didn't, I'd make time for you, Frank. In the six months you've been here, you've made an impact. Our balance sheet finally balances and the flow of cash to the needy has really accelerated."

"Well, it's that flow I wanted to talk about," Frank began. "I've found a few irregularities…"

The smile on Mr. DiAngelo's face froze in place. "What do you mean?"

Frank fiddled with the envelope. He reassured himself that Mr. DiAngelo didn't have anything to do with the envelope's contents. He couldn't know all about the day-to-day operations, especially in the complicated financials.

"Well," Frank said. "I was hired to get the cash flowing more expeditiously, so I've been tracking every dollar we spend." He pulled out a copy of a ledger page with two rows highlighted. He slowly pushed it onto Mr. DiAngelo's desk like it might trip a booby trap. "The two entries I've highlighted are listed as purchases of cleaning supplies."

Mr. DiAngelo peered at the page. "The downtown shelter needs a lot of cleaning."

"But those debits are for $9,500 each, three weeks apart," Frank said. "Nobody uses that much Mr. Clean. And that amount is also just under the government reporting limit. That made me suspicious."

Frank took a deep breath and pulled out a copy of the backs of two cancelled checks. He nudged it over to Mr. DiAngelo.

"This is a copy of the endorsements of the two checks," he said. "Receiving made them out to Woodrow Industrial Supplies.

But if you look at the stamps and account numbers on the back, the bank where they were cashed is in New York City."

"Woodrow could do all their national banking in New York."

"But Woodrow isn't national and the bank account number isn't either," Frank said. "It's international. These checks were cashed by Al Tharwa Aska, an organization in Lebanon."

"I believe that's a humanitarian organization," Mr. DiAngelo said. Any trace of a smile had long since disappeared.

"But its finances are shadowy," Frank said. "A friend of mine with overseas experience says that the government is keeping an eye on it for possible terrorist connections."

Mr. DiAngelo put down the paper. "Thanks for telling me about this, Frank. I'll sit down with the Mary Connelly in Receiving on Monday and get to the bottom of this."

Frank was surprised that Mr. DiAngelo took the news so well. He didn't ask any follow up questions. Maybe he didn't understand the implications for his organization, and for his personal standing.

"I wish that were all," Frank said. He dropped a half dozen more ledger pages on the desk. "I looked for other suspicious transactions over the past year. There are dozens of them, all for amounts just under $10,000. I tracked a number of them to two non-profits in North America."

Mr. DiAngelo had no reaction to the news. Frank sighed. His boss still didn't get it.

"So I looked into the organizations," Frank continued. "They all have overlapping ties, either financial or managerial. One is recorded as being founded in 1850 in Boston to aid Irish immigrants, the other in 1882 to support missionary work in the Southwest. Since both of those causes have long ago disappeared, I'm afraid the organizations are scams."

"So you think someone is stealing?" Mr. DiAngelo said.

"No, I *know* they are," Frank said. "Someone, or more likely a few people, are siphoning off funds from our company to front organizations. It may just be theft, but the money could also be financing drug running, weapons or terrorism. If Sunrise gets caught up in that, your reputation will be ruined, even if you knew nothing about it."

Mr. DiAngelo stood up behind his desk. He gathered Frank's papers and folded them in half. He went to the slit window and stared out at the bricks.

"These are serious accusations," he said. "Your paper trail backs them up?"

"Completely."

"And as a CPA you are bound to report these irregularities to your employer, which you have done," Mr. DiAngelo said. "You would also be bound to report them to the police if we took no action, correct?"

"No, no," Frank said. "Well, yes I would have to, but that won't be necessary. I'll help you find out who's behind this and we'll put an end to it. We won't have to get the government involved."

Mr. DiAngelo turned and looked at Frank's right hand. "I see you are a Knight of Columbus. They do many good works in the name of Christ. What was your most recent project?"

Frank paused at this bizarre change of conversational direction.

"We sponsored a Christmas toy drive," Frank answered with apprehension.

"You understand the rewards of doing good," Mr. DiAngelo said. "That will help. I'll explain a few things to you, Frank. In the end, you tell me what steps we need to take."

Frank leaned back in his chair, a bit afraid that Mr. DiAngelo might be more involved than he had assumed. His boss sat back down at his desk. He gave the papers in his hands another fold.

"Tell me Frank, of the sins outlined in the Ten Commandments, which do you think is the worst?"

Frank wondered where this was going. If it was some rationalization for breaking the law, it wasn't going to wash.

"Murder," Frank said off the top of his head.

"And the most severe punishment for that crime?" Mr. DiAngelo said.

"Death."

"So one would think," Mr. DiAngelo said. He unfolded the papers and laid out the one with the Lebanese transactions. "First let me assure you that Al Tharwa Aska has no terrorist ties. All their money goes to help Maronite Christians in Lebanon, a shrinking minority. I also assure you that I authorized that transfer, however backhanded it might have been."

He unlocked a drawer in the bottom of his desk and pulled out a heavy ledger bound in rich leather. The book smelled musty as an old attic. Stains soiled the wrinkled page edges.

"I am confident of the Lebanon charity's honesty because I own it," Mr. DiAngelo said. "That charity and twenty-nine others, including Sunrise here and the two others you mentioned. Each one supports Christian communities or causes."

He flipped open the ledger and leafed through a few yellowed pages. Each one had a charity name as a heading and figures for annual income, overhead and outlays. Some of the dates were over one hundred fifty years old. Frank thought that this Good Samaritan empire must have been passed down through Mr. DiAngelo's family.

"Here are the bottom line records for each one, the summary P&L to you accountants," Mr. DiAngelo said. "Fundraising ebbs and flows, but never in sync with need. So when we have a banner year here in Miami, I spread the wealth to places with greater need, like Lebanon."

"But we could do that legally," Frank said. "I can show you the forms we need to use, even for overseas transfers."

"I wish I could," Mr. DiAngelo said. "But we have to stay below the radar. Too many charities under one umbrella look suspicious. It looked suspicious to you. Could be a front for a drug cartel, slavery or whatever the sin-of-the-decade fad is."

"I can make sure our organization stands up to financial scrutiny," Frank volunteered.

"I'm sure you could," Mr. DiAngelo said with a slight smile. "But it isn't just Sunrise that needs to stay out from under the microscope. It's me. I'm going to tell you a story that may test the limits of your faith."

Frank sat up a bit straighter in his seat.

"Years ago," Mr. DiAngelo said, "I committed a cardinal sin. Your number one answer, murder, or at the minimum, I was an accomplice to one. As soon as I realized what I had done, I was filled with remorse, like something black and horrible had taken up residence inside me. I knew, as you said, there was only one punishment for my crime. Death. So I tied a noose to a stout tree and hung myself, too stupid to realize I was compounding the sin of murder with the sin of suicide."

Mr. DiAngelo unbuttoned the top two buttons of his shirt and pulled the collar open. An inch-wide purple scar circled his neck. Frank winced.

"The problem was, I didn't die. I blacked out and woke up atop a pile of bodies, other unclaimed corpses waiting for burial. Well, I bolted out of there and went to try it again. And try I did. I threw myself off a cliff, drowned myself in the ocean, even impaled myself. Each time I blacked out and awoke alive and uninjured.

"So Frank, when you say the ultimate penalty for murder is death, I tell you the ultimate penalty is life. Eternal life living with the sin you have committed."

Frank shifted in his chair as the story veered into fantasy.

"Once I accepted that every pain inducing torment I endured wouldn't kill me, I gave up," Mr. DiAngelo said. "I decided to use this interminable life to do good. I would support Christians in need, to atone for my sin. Over the decades I founded charities around the world. This decade, I work from Miami to keep them all in business."

Frank thought about the leather bound book, not passed from person to person over the decades, just annotated by Mr. DiAngelo each year. All the entries *were* in the same handwriting…no, the idea was impossible.

"And you hope your acts will gain you forgiveness?" Frank asked.

"Not in the least," Mr. DiAngelo sighed. "I am beyond redemption. After so many years, so much effort against insatiable demand, I'd be happy to just die and go to Hell."

Frank wasn't a fan of the supernatural. His face betrayed his skepticism for Mr. DiAngelo's story.

"You've seen my handwriting on some impossibly old documents, but you still doubt my story," Mr. DiAngelo said. He stood and spun the dials on a combination lock on the file cabinet behind the desk. The drawer rolled open with a screech and Mr. DiAngelo pulled two fragile photographs from within. He tossed them on the desk.

One showed Frank's boss near the turn of the twentieth-century, helping a rowboat of Turkish Christian refugees landing in Greece during one of the Ottoman purges. The other showed him standing by a tent bearing a red cross. The uniform of the legless soldier next to him dated the picture from the Civil War. "I'm afraid I don't keep a lot of souvenirs, and since the 1860's I've tried to keep out of pictures, but there are these two."

A hobbyist photographer, Frank could spot a fake. He knew the feel of true antique photographic paper. These photos were undeniably real. Frank looked into Mr. DiAngelo's eyes. For the first time he realized how old they looked. Could he really...

"The Bible's full of miracles, Frank," Mr. DiAngelo said. "Don't you believe one when you see one?"

"So, how old are you?" Frank had to ask.

"A lot older than this," Mr. DiAngelo said, giving the leather book a tap.

Frank sat in silence. The scar, the ledger, the pictures. Overwhelming physical evidence lay before him. True faith demanded far less.

"So what should we do about our accounting problem, Frank?"

"I say we forget it," Frank said. "And on Monday, I'll show you a better way to cover your financial tracks."

"I'm glad you understand," Mr. DiAngelo said. "It goes without saying that this conversation is just between us."

"Absolutely."

"Then go before you are late for Holy Thursday Mass, Knight. We'll discuss this more Monday morning."

Frank collected himself as best he could. He gave Mr. DiAngelo a nod and left his office. He stopped in the doorway for one last question.

"What was your sin?"

Mr. DiAngelo stared out at the brick wall again, but Frank knew he was looking uncounted miles and years away.

"I arranged the execution of my best friend," he said, "for thirty pieces of silver."

Ω

Road Warriors

Eighteen miles to Kingman. He tingled with anticipation.

Earl Bagwell shifted in the driver's seat of his Freightliner Coronado as it rolled down I-40. The big Detroit diesel under the hood loafed along as it pulled a trailer full of eggs that cubed out the load thousands of pounds under the big rig's max. The bright headlights pierced the darkness a thousand yards out and illuminated acres of stunted desert scrub. Earl lit his twelfth cigarette of the hour, a new record.

These wee hours were prime trucker time for doing the long haul routes. Commuters and vacationing families abandoned the roads at night, and the tar and concrete became the domain of the rolling colossi. Cops were scarce, and you could detour around the weigh stations without anyone noticing. At no other time could you blow across Phoenix in under twenty minutes.

Thousands strong, linked by CB and Sirius Radio, the travelling brotherhood shared the night, a subculture of secret slang and shared stimulants, who operated off the radar of the average American. Earl loved to work in this world, a world primed for the hunt.

Earl rolled down his window. Hot desert air blasted his face like a nuclear hair dryer. The smell of asphalt wafted into the cabin, still cooking after a day in the scorching desert sun. He flicked the stub of his cigarette into the darkness. The wind blew across his gray, stubbled buzz cut, a style unchanged for the last ten of his fifty years. His glasses had grown cool in the truck's air conditioning, and the warm air fogged them over. He pulled a red bandana from the dashboard and wiped them dry.

Normally, it was tough to stay awake through the stretch between three AM and four AM. But Earl needed no chemical assistance this evening. His blood ran hot. His heart thudded fast and hard. It was time to start stalking prey.

His quarry would be waiting in Kingman, though that was just one of hundreds of places. Kingman's Trans-American Truck Stop attracted them like moths to a halogen spotlight. These hours were their prime feeding time, arriving like mosquitoes to suck the blood of arriving victims. Truckers called them lot lizards. Earl called them whores.

His mother had taught him early and often about the evils of sex. How dirty it was, the diseases you could catch. His mother's one experience with it at eighteen had gotten her knocked up and abandoned by the father Earl never knew. Then her preachy parents threw her out of the house, and she was on her own. All her problems started with sex.

These women who sold themselves to strangers disgusted Earl. A filthy act, committed by filthy people. The idea of it made his skin crawl. The truck stop whores were nothing more than rats that needed extermination. For the last decade, he'd been doing the decent world a favor.

A billboard advertising the Trans-American passed by. Next exit. Five miles. Clean restrooms. Open 24 hours.

Earl had been there before, but not to hunt. He was careful where he killed. Never the same place twice. Never the same state twice in a row. He kept a mental list of locations he'd scouted across the country, and then worked through the list as he crisscrossed the nation.

The yellow signage of the Trans-American peeked over the horizon, advertising the diesel oasis. Earl guided his rig up the exit ramp, and into the truck stop. A faded convenience store sat off the main road with two wings of fuel pumps; a low roof over the gasoline pumps to the right, a higher one for the diesel on the left. Earl wheeled around to the acres of parking lot behind the store.

Streetlamps lit the lot in a pinkish neon light that gave everything the texture of cotton candy. A dozen rigs lined up under the lights. Half were traveling billboards for Big Macs, Doritos and Wal-Mart. An orange, midsize U-Haul sat parked a few rows over, like a kid brother to the larger pro rigs, not quite able to step up with the bigger boys. No doubt that driver was sleeping the night away. The ones in the rigs were not.

The women buzzed around the trucks like flies over carrion. They hawked meth, speed, and of course, themselves. They wore cheap, clingy clothes that advertised their sagging breasts and expanded thighs. The hazy lot lighting assisted the heavy makeup and thick eyeliner in concealing the years and hard miles on their faces. But when they stepped into the brighter light of a trucker's cab, the cheap cosmetics painted them as ghastly clowns.

Earl parked his rig at the end of the row, leaving a few spaces between his truck and the next. He flipped on the lights in the sleeper. The extended cab behind his seat had a single bunk, some faux wood shelving and a black privacy curtain to separate it from any prying eyes though the windshield. Earl did his best work behind that curtain.

He began the ritual. He checked the pistol in the glove box. Bullets gleamed in the magazine, each dipped in holy water. He snapped the magazine in place and chambered a round. He pulled a new, expendable white sheet from the shelf and spread it over the bunk, so that nothing touched by the creature he invited in would ever touch him. He opened a bottle of chloroform, poured it in a shallow Tupperware dish, tossed a rag on top and slid the dish's lid into place. He put the container on the shelf over the bunk.

Once she lay down to do whatever disgusting deed she had offered, he used the chloroform to knock her unconscious. A short drive through the desert, and one bullet rid the world of another twisted daughter of Sodom. The proof that he was doing society a favor was that no one ever noticed when the sluts were missing. There were never any news stories, never any anguished fliers in the truck stop windows. He was just slapping society's mosquitoes.

He returned to the driver's seat and surveyed the lot. Two skanks eyed the truck like wolves. They teetered toward him in their cheap, high heels. He felt that shameful bulge in his pants grow, the one his mother told him was so evil. But it wasn't their services that aroused him. It was the service he'd be providing for one of them.

He flicked his windshield wipers once across the windshield. The women retreated at this universal wave-off. Earl knew not to hunt in the pack. A witness was the last thing he wanted when one of them entered his cab. He hunted the loner, the one who could vanish without a trace.

A girl exited one of the cabs down the row. She adjusted her shorts as she hit the ground. She walked away, her ass swinging like a pendulum with each retreating step.

Earl's skin crawled as he imagined the revolting act she'd just performed. He did not understand this preoccupation with sex.

His mother had explained the sick act to him. On his fourteenth birthday, she even took him into her bed and guided him through each step of it with her, so he could see how repulsive it was. His climax had been so revolting, he'd nearly thrown up.

A lone woman walked around the rear of one of the trucks. She wore cut-off jean shorts and a T-shirt with broad red and white stripes. A cheap, floppy black bag hung at one shoulder. Her hair was a platinum blonde, shoulder length with bangs. Earl thought it looked like a wig, which made her twice the slut. His pulse quickened.

She seemed to check the Arizona plates on the other rig, and then looked over at Earl's. She smiled and swaggered in his direction. Earl rolled down the passenger side window. She mounted the running boards. She grasped the window opening with both hands. Earl stifled a cringe. He'd have to sanitize that. She peered in through the window

"I'm Harley," she said. Her face was heavily painted, though in less desperate need of it than most lot lizards. "You looking for some fun?" She had a slow, white trash Georgia drawl.

"You bet," Earl said.

Harley looked down at his swollen Levi's. The parking lot lights backlit her hair like an incongruous halo. "Looks like you are cocked and ready, stud."

Earl's face went red, embarrassed and infuriated by this whore's casual allusion to his humiliating display.

"Don't be shy about it, hon," Harley said. "How do you want it? A quick blow for twenty-five or the full ride for a hundred?"

Earl plastered on an enticing smile. "Let's have a real party for a hundred." He pulled a rumpled hundred dollar bill from his pocket and laid it on the console by his seat. The same bill had passed through the hands of dozens of tramps on their last night on earth. "C'mon in."

Harley popped open the door. She climbed up and into the sleeper. She palmed the C note as she passed. The cheap stink of some knockoff perfume blanketed him. He imagined the disgusting odors the scent masked. This whore's death would so help cleanse the world.

Earl's heart pounded like a bass drum as he took a quick scan of the parking lot. Empty. Witness count: zero. Perfect.

Harley tossed her purse on the bunk and sat down. She splayed her legs apart. "Let's get it on, hon."

Earl entered the sleeper. Her escape route was sealed. The cab would deaden any screams she might make. From this moment on, she was all his. He looked into her eyes and sprouted a grisly smile. He turned away and pulled the privacy curtain shut.

White, electric pain shot up from the base of his spine and exploded into his skull. His body spasmed violently and his glasses flew across the cabin. Just as the charge ebbed, a second wave crashed through his body. He swore his brain would boil. He pissed his jeans. His knees went weak as his head swam. He dropped and flopped back against the bunk.

Harley stood over him, a stun gun in her left hand. Her eyes blazed in vengeful triumph.

"So you want a little action, asshole," she said. The Georgia accent was gone, replaced by a thick, natural one from New York. "Just a quick fuck while you're away from the wife and kids?" She jammed the stun gun into his groin and fired.

His balls caught fire. Earl shrieked in pain. The charge subsided. Every sinew in his body felt like singed meat. He tried to sit up, but his jellied muscles refused the command, and left him at the mercy of this psycho whore.

Harley pulled a roll of silver duct tape from her bag. She grabbed Earl by the hair and yanked his head off the floor. She wrapped a band of tape over his mouth and around his head. Then she bound his hands and feet together until he was trussed up like a calf awaiting branding.

She knelt down and thrust her face next to Earl's. With his glasses gone, this close up, she became a tan blur with dark recesses for eyes. "It's all rape you know," she hissed. "Whether you pay for it, or whether you think we're consenting. We're not. It's all we can do to keep from puking at the thought of touching you."

What the hell was this? he thought. *Who was this bitch?*

She kicked Earl hard in the ribs. He screamed into the duct tape. He had to inhale in short, sharp draws through his nose, and feared he was going to suffocate.

Harley stood and towered over Earl. She slipped off her wig. Her left ear was just a pink jagged edge. Her shaved head carried a pattern of deep purple scars that crisscrossed her scalp.

"This is your work, you rapist pig. You and the rest of your revolting gender. Take a good look at the crime you'll pay for."

That wasn't his work. He'd never seen this lunatic before.

The privacy curtain snapped back into place as Harley left the sleeper. Earl lay on the floor of his truck, soaked in his own urine and immobilized by yards of duct tape. One tug against his restraints confirmed that escape would be impossible. Powerless and controlled by a woman, his greatest fears realized. He struggled for breath, and tears welled in his eyes.

The rig slid into first and crept through the parking lot. It was a perfect launch, without a buck or shudder from the big truck, as if Harley had driven one of these before.

◆◆◆

Two days later, Arizona Trooper Don McNeese sat in his cruiser, parked in the baking sun in a vacant lot outside Winona. Earl's Freightliner sat a dozen yards away, decidedly downwind. The load of rotten eggs in the trailer had an aroma best avoided. Both doors of the abandoned truck hung open after the trooper's search.

"Driver was one Earl Bagwell," he said to his sergeant on the other end of his cell phone. He looked over the registration pulled from the cab. "Florida address. The vendor on his manifest says he's a day overdue delivering the load of eggs in his trailer. My nose testifies that they are at least a day past ripe."

"Any sign of him?" the sergeant asked.

"Nope," Trooper McNichol said. "Cab's clean and tidy. Rig's a quarter mile from a c-store, so he could have walked there for help if he had a problem. No one there saw him. Looks like he just abandoned his rig."

"Third one this month on I-40," the sergeant answered. "Drivers fall behind on payments, and just walk away and start a new life."

"This economy is hell," the trooper said.

Ω

Dark Vengeance Sample

Will the blood of innocents release an evil entity near Galaxy Farm?

A coven of witches has moved into the tiny town near Galaxy Farm. They know about a dormant evil entity, and they hope to resurrect it and set it free to renew its hunt of mankind. All they need for their sacrifices is the blood of innocent children. Only Laura Locke and Theresa Grissom have the skills to defeat this supernatural danger, but their previous brush with the evil at Galaxy Farm has shattered their relationship. If they can't work together to stop the coven in time, hundreds will die. Starting with Theresa's son.

Chapter One

The fire left little of Galaxy Farm.

Only the old barn still stood. The glass in the central cupola reflected the moonlight like some low-output lighthouse. Three deaths had occurred in there: the sheriff, the crazy writer and Vern Pugh. Stories of barn hauntings already circulated throughout the nearby small town of Moultrie, Tennessee. Even before the fire took the main house, the triple homicide had sparked stories of the barn being haunted. Everyone in the nearby small town of Moultrie, Tennessee, accepted the tales as fact.

Later, the foreboding barn would no doubt be where the kids would go. Middle school boys on a dare. High school teens on a date. The only structure left on the fifteen acres would draw them all.

But the willowy woman who moved through the night didn't give the barn a thought. She trudged up the long gravel drive to the ruins of the once-proud home. Three of the walls on the first floor still stood. Their ragged, burned edges were all that hinted an upper story had existed. That second story, and all that had been above it, now lay in a charred heap in the house's open interior. Twenty-four hours after the blaze, the remains were cool, but the humid air was still redolent with the conflagration's acrid smell.

The woman crossed the remnants of the front porch. The boards creaked with each hesitant step. There was no telling how badly the fire had damaged the joists below. Her research confirmed that the house had no basement, but even a short fall through to the foundation could break a bone.

Her long, open black duster flicked the edge of the gaping front doorway as she entered the house's dead shell. Mounds of shadowy remains covered the floor. Jagged, broken rafters jutted from the pile like limbs of the dead in rigor mortis. Now shielded from the prying eyes driving along nearby US 41, she flicked on a penlight.

She played the bright, narrow beam across the wreckage. The legacy of the long-dead previous owner, Mabron Hutchington, would still be here somewhere. None of his supernatural works ever left the house after his death, not when his brother owned it afterwards, not when his nephew Vern inherited it and certainly not when Doug and Laura Locke had moved in last year. A tiny rural-Tennessee town like Moultrie would know.

Mabron had practiced his brand of dark magic here for years. It was Egyptian-tinged, but parallel to her own, tapping the same great sources of natural power.

She pulled aside a blackened board. Yellow eyes and a set of bared white canines flashed in the penlight's beam. Her heart skipped a beat and she stumbled backwards against a wall.

The teeth did not move. She panned the light around them and lit a wolf's head, long dead, taxidermied for eternal preservation. But the fire had seared away its hide and left just a blackened, clay-infused skull, two marble eyes and the menacing teeth.

She smiled at the welcome sign, a part of Mabron's extensive collection of magic-infused taxidermy. When the house went up in flames the night before, Mabron's possessed possessions had indeed still been here.

She moved the penlight to her mouth to free up her hands. Tossing aside some boards, she uncovered a collapsed wooden chest. She pried open the warped lid. A stack of charred papers, perhaps once books, filled one side. They disintegrated at her touch, as if whatever magic they once relayed wanted to stay out of her reach.

On the other side sat a collection of glass eyes, all sizes and colors. Each gazed off in a different direction, like a cyclopean swarm in search of an escape.

These tempted her, but they were unused. A proper talisman had to have already been infused with magic, already begun on that difficult path between the world of reality and the one that pulsed just under reality's surface. The wolf's glass eyes perhaps would do, but they carried a low residual charge. The optimal piece would be a personal item, something Mabron had kept close to him while he cast the spells he'd used to keep souls barred from the hereafter. Perhaps a ring, a watch, a pair of glasses.

She pawed through the rest of the cinders in the box and found nothing. She turned and shined her light into what had been the living room. A flash of silver winked at her from within a recess in the debris. She picked her way across the unstable wreckage and knelt at the location.

She pulled off her glove and reached blindly into the small space. Her fingertips tingled. Her pulse skipped a beat. She sensed that this object that called to her from across the ruined house was rich with magic. It had not been an object of it, but instead continually exposed to it, like iron magnetized by passing through an electric field. The house fire's residual heat rose and enveloped her arm as she reached deeper into the debris. Her fingers touched cold metal and she snatched it.

She opened her fist in her flashlight's bright glow and revealed a silver locket. Its delicate, detailed turn-of-the-century engraving implied it had been a woman's, but the aura it exuded left no doubt that Mabron wore it during his most intense magic spells.

She popped it open. Ashes were all that remained of the pictures inside, as if whoever the locket had immortalized had fully passed from this world. But that did not matter. The magic mattered. And with its previous prolonged exposure, this talisman would be powerful indeed.

She snapped off her light and buried her treasure in her front pocket. She thought better of that and placed the chain around her neck. She flipped her long hair outside the chain and tucked the locket into her shirt. It nestled between her breasts.

From atop the barn, an owl puffed out two shrill hoots, as if warning that it was time to depart.

She hopped across the house's remains and through the missing front door. Her open coat flew behind her like a cape as she broke into a run back to her car. With each stride, the locket bounced against her chest, little taps timed like a countdown clock on the greatest spell her coven would ever cast.

Ω

Dreamwalker Sample

What if you lived in two worlds, but could die in either?

College freshman Pete Holm can. He is a dreamwalker, one gifted in traveling to the realm of dreams. There he finds the devastated world of Twin Moon City, a place where the evil voodoo spirit of Cauquemere holds trapped souls at bay with his army of the walking dead.

In the waking world, Pete becomes enmeshed in the Atlantic City drug empire of Jean St Croix, a psychopath on the verge of completing a deal that will consolidate his hold on the heroin trade in a tri-state bloodbath. St. Croix knows that Pete is the only one with the power to stop him.

The clock ticks as Pete must do what only he can, rescue the lost souls in Twin Moon City and cut short the earthly reign of St. Croix. In the balance hangs Rayna, the captivating girl from his dreams. Is she real or imagined, and can they have a future together when all this is over?

Chapter One

Flaming arrows sang by Pete's ears, one so close the heat singed his hair. A quick glance over his shoulder revealed a horde of tribesmen closing fast from the edge of the jungle clearing. They wore animal skin loincloths with bizarre fur patterns. Necklaces of human teeth pounded against their tanned chests as they charged. In unison, they screamed like shearing metal and displayed mouths full of tiger shark teeth. The lead savage, face painted white as death, brandished a trident with a man's gaping skull on each tine.

Pete's instant arrival here wasn't the least disorienting. In a flash, his memory gaps filled in. A magic emerald figurine sat heavy in the pouch at his waist. When he and his team took it across the rope bridge over the gorge, the spells the leader had cast over the local villages would be broken.

Three of them were running to the bridge, one man yards ahead and almost there. He was familiar yet somehow nameless, the same late-teen age as Pete, clad in similar khaki shorts and a grimy t-shirt. Sunlight flashed off a tortoise shell shield slung across his shoulder. He reached the anchors of the rickety suspension bridge and spun around. He unshouldered the shield. Wind from the gorge behind him blew his brown hair back across his face. He crouched to defend the rope bridge entrance.

"Pete, hurry!"

Pete instinctively glanced back to check for her. She was right on Pete's heels, her footfalls in sync with his. Her long blonde hair trailed behind her, a hint of panic in her green eyes. Even mottled with the jungle's dirt, her graceful features were beautiful. That's why she was Dream Girl.

"I'm here," she panted. "Don't wait."

The tribesmen's scream came louder this time as they closed the gap. Another volley of burning arrows cut the air. Several stuck into the suspension bridge planks. Pete hit the bridge at full speed, hands gliding along the gnarled rope railing. The blonde was right behind him.

They were halfway across when Pete heard the scream. He could only get a glimpse past his shoulder, but that was enough. A shield pierced with flaming arrows. A lifeless body on the ground. Men with machetes chopped at the ropes.

"Don't look back," he yelled. "Run!"

The hand railing ropes jumped in sync with the hack of each tribesman's machete. The bridge bounced as they bounded down the last few feet. Pete leapt across the remaining planks and landed on the far side of the gorge. The sickening crack of rotted wood rolled across from the gorge's other side.

Pete whirled around. The log towers at the far end tore from the ground and tumbled into the expanse. Parted twin support ropes flew towards him like snapped rubber bands. The bridge dropped. Dream Girl's determined look turned into shock as the planks fell away beneath her.

"Pete!"

Pete's hand darted out and grabbed her arm. He wrapped his other arm around one tower's base log. Her hand gripped his wrist. It was soft, but strong. She looked up with a smile of relief.

"A bit too close, don't you think?" she said.

Then it all dissolved, that episode over.

Pete Holm spent his nights this way, bouncing from dream to dream. They were usually great adventures, Hollywood blockbusters inside his head as he sailed pirate ships or fought off space aliens. While most people had fuzzy dreams with muddled narratives, Pete dreamed with exceptional clarity. Technicolor hues, exquisite detail, nuanced scents. He'd describe it as more real than reality, if there was someone he'd ever describe it to. And while most people's dreams faded with the advance of consciousness, Pete's remained sharp as high definition TV.

But the real nightly treats were continuing storylines. His dreams often picked up the next evening where they left off. And while Pete might start *in media res,* as his English professor described certain stories, he knew exactly where he was and what he was doing, as if he'd just paused the movie from the night before. Characters rarely made the transition from one storyline to the next, except for Dream Girl, the forever unnamed beautiful blonde with the emerald eyes.

He was always aware that he was dreaming, but knowing that never made it any less real, any more than a pilot in a flight simulator ever felt like he wasn't flying. He regretted that he lacked control of the dream's outcome, a prerogative his subconscious refused to yield.

In tonight's double feature, he now stood alone in what he had dubbed The Mansion, a brick antebellum masterpiece, complete with an immense two story front porch. The house had been with him his entire life, a slowly evolving symbol of Southern graciousness. A warm sense of recognition filled him upon each arrival.

Pete stood at the base of a staircase that rivaled Tara's, stretching to the unfinished second floor. Ornate trim work surrounded each door in the room and the dark wood floor was waxed to a mirror finish. Paintings of places Pete had visited and loved hung on the walls, scenes like Niagara Falls and the backyard of his grandmother's house. The open front doors ushered in a breeze touched with the invigorating scent of fresh-cut alfalfa.

Some things in the mansion changed with each visit, some always remained the same. The second floor never altered, forever a maze of rough framed walls and plywood flooring. Old-fashioned copper stubs of incomplete plumbing poked through the floors and errant pigtailed wires sprouted from the wall studs. Pete had plans for the expanse on the second floor; a room with a pool table, a master bedroom with a veranda, a bathroom with an archaic claw foot tub. One night he would arrive, and the new rooms would be finished.

On the ground floor, hallways snaked away in impossible lengths, promising yet more undiscovered spaces. Through each door, some rooms were familiar, some not. Often first floor rooms were empty, though they had been furnished in other visits. Pete peered inside a few doors, rediscovering the mansion, finding details his subconscious had added.

Pete entered his favorite room, an elegant sunroom, with three walls and a ceiling of solid glass panels in a wrought iron frame. Potted tropical plants covered the floor, parting to make a path to an open observation area. Daylight blazed down on the white marble floor. Through the glass, a lush green lawn rolled away from the mansion. Pete decided to spend the dream right here, warmed by the sun and bathed in the scents of rich earth and flowering plants.

Suddenly something ice cold blew through him, like an Arctic blast that penetrated his clothes, his skin, his soul. He shivered. His stomach clenched in an involuntary knot of fear.

A low rumbling noise rolled across the vast stretch of lawn, like the roar of a distant jet. At the far edge of the grass, a dark, amorphous mass emerged from the trees. The pulsating mix of black smoke and grey substance nosed out into the open. It slithered across the grass like a huge worm and began a slow zigzag up the hill to the mansion.

Pete stepped to the window and gripped the cold iron window pane. His short, shallow breaths fogged the glass.

The apparition closed on the house. Its bellowing's pitch grew piercing and shrill. It probed Pete's head like steel needles. He covered his ears.

The creature sharpened into a massive grey snake, a freight train of shifting scales with jagged spikes along its back. The head reared up. A gaunt shadowy face, as misshapen as a Picasso abstract, stared through the window at Pete with empty black eye sockets. Its mouth stretched into a howling oval. The head wore a peaked officer's cap with an indistinct central white logo. Around its neck hung a tarnished medallion on a thick chain. It bore the likeness of two crossed snakes, one dark and one light.

It slithered back and forth across the yard ever quicker, but its gaze never wavered. It remained locked on the mansion, the head swiveling counter to the body movement, always facing the sunroom, always facing Pete.

Pete staggered back from the glass. This was all wrong. He was in *the mansion*. Mansion dreams were never nightmares. What was this thing he summoned that came on like a killer entering a schoolyard?

The creature turned again, and charged the sunroom. The hideous head closed on the mansion. Its ear-shattering shriek pierced Pete's skull. The hairs on his arms stood on end and vibrated in time with the creature's wailing. The white object on the peak of the cap came into focus, a clenched skeletal fist.

Its pit of a mouth opened wider, as if to ingest the house. Windowpanes in the house shuddered from the screaming noise. Pete fell to his knees. His heart slammed inside his chest.

Pete's subconscious reached up, grabbed a hold of the real world, and pulled.

He woke up in his dark dorm room in a cold, soaking sweat. He clenched the edge of the bed and prayed it was really over. His roommate snored. Pete relaxed and slumped back into his pillow. The clock read 4:50 am.

This is no way to start the first day of midterm exams, he thought.

Ω Ω

Want more short stories?

Try *Dust and Bones.*

Russell James delivers a new collection of horror and suspense short stories in *Dust and Bones*. This collection has all these thrillers set in the past. Some of the tales include:

- In the frontier West, a prostitute meets a rich client, and sees her ticket to a life of leisure. What unfolds for her is something completely different.
- A World War I pilot flies into a strange cloud, and exits into World War II.
- Signing aboard a sailing ship plying the slave trade in the 1800s seems like a great adventure for one young man, but horrors beyond imagination await him and the entire crew.
- During the Civil War, Union Army deserters arrive to ransack a plantation mansion. The doctor they encounter within makes them wish they had never left camp.

These and ten more shadowy stories from the past wait within the covers of *Dust and Bone*. Available on Amazon in Kindle and paperback.

Russell James

About the Author

Russell James grew up on Long Island, New York and spent too much time watching late night horror. After flying helicopters with the U.S. Army and a career as a technical writer, he now spins twisted tales best read in daylight, including horror thrillers *Dark Inspiration, Q Island,* and *The Playing Card Killer.* He authored the Grant Coleman Adventures series starting with *Cavern of the Damned*, the Rick and Rose Sinclair Adventures series starting with *Quest for the Queen's Temple*, and the Ranger Kathy West Adventures series starting with *Claws.*

He resides in sunny Florida. His wife reads his work, rolls her eyes, and says "There is something seriously wrong with you."

They share their home in sunny Florida with Timothy, a red tabby who has written his own book.

More free short stories are available at www.russellrjames.com.

Drop a line to denigrate his writing at rrj@russellrjames.com.

Facebook at http://www.facebook.com/pages/Russell-R-James/172907172791996.

Follow on Twitter @RRJames14 or rrjames14 on Instagram.

Russell James

Made in the USA
Middletown, DE
23 November 2025

21177059R00076